PATRIOT OF THE UNDERGROUND

Hitler's panzer divisions shattered France in May and June of 1940. For five years France was occupied, but never fully conquered. French men, French women, and French boys continued to wage war against the Nazis.

In the small mining towns of northeastern France, boys worked in the mines from their pre-teen days, taking the same risks as did adults. When the Nazis seized the men for slave labor elsewhere, or as retaliation for the sabotage of the Resistance, many boys in their lower teens joined the underground movement.

This is the story of a group of French boys, led by Paul La Coque. The fathers of Paul and some friends have been seized. The boys know their elders were members of the Resistance, and soon are able to contact the leaders of the movement and volunteer for help. How the boys come to realize what underground work really entails makes exciting reading.

PATRIOT *of the* UNDERGROUND

by Robin McKown

**Illustrated by
EDNA KAULA**

G. P. Putnam's Sons   New York

Fourth Impression

© 1964 by Robin McKown
All rights reserved
Library of Congress Catalog Card Number: 64–13047

Manufactured in the United States of America
Published simultaneously in the Dominion of Canada
by Longmans Canada Limited, Toronto
10214

CONTENTS

*To Jean and Madeleine
Whose patriotic activities
inspired this story*

FOREWORD

On September 1, 1939, German troops invaded Poland on orders from Adolf Hitler. Two days later France and England declared war on Germany. World War II had officially begun. Many millions would die before the conflict was settled. A sea of tears would be shed. And heroic deeds beyond calculation would be performed.

The year before, September 30, 1938, the heads of the French and English governments had signed the Munich Pact, granting to Germany the Sudetenland, a strip of mountainous country in northern Czechoslovakia. The excuse for this betrayal of Czechoslovakia was that the Pact would "appease" Hitler and end his acts of aggression. Ever since, "Munich" and "appeasement" have been synonymous in popular speech. It did not work. In March of 1939 the Germans occupied all of Czechoslovakia. With the attack on Poland, it was clear that the Nazis could not be appeased.

The word "Nazi" is an abbreviation for the National Socialist German Workers' Party, originally a small group of dissatisfied white-collar workers. Hitler joined them in the early 1920's. With them he launched his shameful political career. Under his ministrations, the Nazis grew powerful. In 1933, Hitler became Chancellor of Germany, and shortly thereafter had made himself sole dictator. "Nazi" became a symbol for all that is evil—for brutality and cynicism, wholesale robbery and pillage, for suppression of human and civil rights, race prejudice and mass murder.

It took the Nazis just nine days to conquer Poland. Another word was added to the universal vocabulary—*blitzkrieg,* meaning a lightning attack.

The winter of 1939–1940 passed with comparative calm. The English blockaded the Germans by sea. The French, at least some of them, were lulled to a false sense of security because of the massive fortifications of the Maginot Line, stretching some two hundred miles along their border between Belgium and Switzerland. This was the period known as the "phony war," which the French called *"une drôle de guerre,"* a droll war. "The German is a dog which barks but does not bite," the French radio blasted.

The "phony war" ended abruptly on April 8, 1940, when German troops launched *blitzkriegs* against Norway and Denmark. On May 10, they overran tiny Luxembourg and invaded Holland and Belgium, leaving death, destruction and terror. On May 11, they marched into France from Belgium, skirting around the Maginot Line, which proved without value. They entered Paris on June 10, and twelve days later, Marshal Philippe Pétain, Premier of France, signed an ignominious armistice with Hitler. The French people wept with despair and bitterness, realizing they had been betrayed by their own leaders. The French Government then moved south from Paris to the town of Vichy. Another new word was created—"Vichy," referring to French who collaborated with the Nazis.

Back in 1925, Hitler had written a book called *Mein Kampf* (My Struggle), outlining his plan for European conquest. At the time most sensible people dismissed the book as the ravings of a madman. Now he was well on his way to completing that conquest. His armies seemed invincible.

But not even bombs and bullets can make willing slaves of free men. In all the occupied countries there were rumblings of resentment. People gathered secretly in their homes or elsewhere. In big cities and country villages, in the mountain regions and on the coast, in factories and on farms, an underground Resistance movement sprang into being.

This story is set in a small mining town in northeastern France, a bleak region unfamiliar to foreign tourists. Though fiction, it is based on fact. The description of life under Nazi Occupation is drawn from the testimony of many individuals who lived through it. It was not uncommon for youths like Paul La Coque and his friends to take part in clandestine warfare. The types of sabotage mentioned actually took place. A German underground hospital, dating to the First World War, was found by some boys playing in the fields, and there have been discoveries of more ancient subterranean passageways. The bravery of those who risked death and torture and the security of their families to fight for what they believed, is in no way exaggerated.

The Resistance, wherever it existed, is history now, a particularly thrilling kind of history that will long inspire future generations. Though we tell but one small slice of it, we hope it will give our readers an idea of what it was like for a freedom-loving people to live under the yoke of a foreign invader.

CHAPTER 1

THE ARREST

"*Hsst!* The Boches!" Paul spotted them up the path next to the wall surrounding the mines—two young privates, big and blond and rosy-cheeked, out for a stroll.

He and his four youthful companions exchanged quick glances and drew closely together, with Paul and Roland in the lead and the other three smaller boys, Carlo, Gaston, and Jeannot, just behind them.

As the Germans came nearer, it struck Paul that they looked lonesome. No wonder. It could not be pleasant for them, stationed far from their homes and families in this bleak industrial region of Pas de Calais, in France, where nobody wanted them. He felt almost sorry for them, until he reminded himself that though the privates were not so arrogant as the Nazi officers, they were still the enemy and not to be trusted.

The soldiers stopped in front of them, and one of them said in his funny Teutonic accent, "Good day, my boys."

"*Bonjour,* messieurs," they muttered, with the same indifferent politeness their parents adopted toward the occupation forces.

Smiling uncertainly, the Germans continued to stand there, blocking the path. "Me, I have little brother your age." It was the same one who had spoken before. "At home we play football. You like we play football with you sometime?"

"I no understand," said Paul, gravely imitating the man's accent.

"I your friend." The soldier's voice was pleading. "Like boys very much. Understand now?"

"I like you too," Paul answered in patois, the local dialect spoken by the miners. "I like you as much as I like a big fat caterpillar, the kind I squash with my foot. Does that please you?"

"Goot, goot!" The German nodded, obviously unwilling to admit that his school French was not up to this emergency. "We play football, no?"

"We play football, yes," broke in Roland, Paul's closest friend, a husky youth with tousled blond hair. He suddenly brought out the ball which he had concealed behind his back and made a feint of kicking it. "You will be the ball," he said in rapid patois. "We give you a kick, a hard one, and you fly back all the way across the Rhine."

"Goot, goot!" the German repeated, beaming happily. "We play this game soon?"

"The sooner the better," Paul promised cheerfully. "*Au revoir*, messieurs."

All of them filed by, breaking into an exaggerated goose step as they did so.

Paul looked back and saw the Germans staring after them with a puzzled expression, perhaps suspecting that their attempt to be friends had failed. As soon as they were out of sight, the boys' repressed laughter exploded.

"Big fat caterpillars, we will kick you all the way across the Rhine," burst out Gaston, gasping.

"Let's serenade them," suggested Roland. By mutual accord, as they tramped on, they chanted a senseless ditty:

"The regiment of Pure White Cheese
  Fought Camembert in battle long;
  The Port-Salut refused to shoot;
  'Rochefort,' they said, 'you smell too strong.' "

"I wonder how they'll interpret that stirring melody." Gaston, a sandy-haired youth with mischievous eyes, choked with laughter. They had reached their destination, the deserted stadium back of the mines which served them as a football practice field, and they all plopped down unceremoniously on the bare soot-covered ground.

"No doubt they'll think it's a love song," said Carlo, yawning. "The Germans claim that we French are mad about love." There was a certain pride in the way Carlo said "we French." As his olive skin and Roman features indicated, he was of Italian birth. His anti-Fascist father had fled Mussolini's Italy with his family ten years before to work for the French railroads. Their adopted land had been good to them until the war came. Now Carlo considered it his own.

"We French"—Roland made a wry grimace—"we French are not here to discuss the Germans. Let's forget they exist. At least for this afternoon."

Paul nodded soberly. It was September of 1941, some sixteen months after the Nazis, like a plague of hungry locusts, had swarmed over their beloved country. To mock a couple of soldiers might temporarily relieve tension and anger, but Roland was right. One should not think about them all the time.

With a leap he was on his feet. "I'm the goalkeeper," he cried out, swooping down to grab the ball which Roland had let fall to the ground. "Ready. Get set . . ."

With a kick he sent the ball shooting down the field. The others scrambled after it in a flash, kicking it from one to another, using their bodies and their heads in addition to their feet to bat it back and forth, experimenting with the techniques of footwork and dribbling which they had learned from their town's professionals, shouting and yelling to each other all the while.

They continued until the autumn sun approached the horizon. With a sudden feint, Paul, pretending to kick the ball forward to Gaston, slid his foot out and sent it scooting off sideways to where Carlo was standing. The others were on top of it in a moment. Paul joined with them and then they were all down on the ground in an untidy and breathless heap.

They disentangled themselves but made no effort to rise. Dusky from the inevitable coal dust of the mines, sweating and disheveled and exhausted, they could only sit and look at each other and laugh—Paul, a lithe quick-moving youth with brown hair and eyes; Roland; Gaston; the Italian lad, Carlo—and lastly, little Jean, whom they affectionately called Jeannot, the smallest of them all, a boy with an intelligent, sensitive face, wide blue eyes and delicate chiseled features.

"We're getting good," bragged Carlo when he caught his breath.

"Sure," agreed Roland sarcastically. "Maybe the American Government would just send us passage money to play with one of their teams."

"You should know that the Americans do not play football as we do," Gaston said, with a slightly superior air. He had a great-uncle who had once lived in Pittsburgh and was therefore an authority on everything American. "They call our game soccer"—he pronounced it *sock-care*—"not football. Their football is bigger than ours, not round but oval like an egg. And they not only kick it, they throw it."

"They do?" Roland shrugged in mock resignation. "Well, I don't really want to go to America anyway. At least not much."

"Remember when we were small and used to play cowboys and Indians?" Paul reminisced. "I was always Buffalo Bill."

Jeannot sighed wistfully. "It must be great fun to live in America."

"No more than anywhere else," Gaston assured them. "The Americans are no longer at war with the Indians."

The others were not wholly convinced. Their image of America, derived from the films they had seen in their town's one motion picture house, was a kaleidoscope of Indians in feathered headdresses riding ponies across the plains, cowboys with revolvers in hip holsters, and gangsters from Chicago. In every respect, it was in vivid contrast to the drabness of their own lives under German rule. It occurred to none of them that in America there might be youths of their own age who longed to be old enough for the adventure of fighting the Nazis.

Gaston jumped to his feet. "Go to America, if you like. I have to get home or there will be trouble."

The others followed his example. They walked back toward town, a bedraggled crew in their worn and faded pullovers and patched trousers, and pale, once the flush of their sport wore off, like all young people of the black country, as the mining region of France is known.

"This exercise has given me a bit of an appetite," Gaston

announced, his eyes darting from one to another, gauging their reactions. "I think I'll have Mother roast a chicken for my supper. In butter."

They were all ravenous, a permanent state since the coming of the Germans, and joined readily in Gaston's game of make-believe.

"I'll have two chickens, waiter." Roland spoke in the tone of a gentleman placing an order in a restaurant. "After that a roast beef. With a platter of fried potatoes."

"We'll start with *hors d'oeuvres,*" said Jeannot gleefully. "Waiter, a dozen eggs stuffed with mayonnaise and lobster, a plate of cold cuts, some olives, radishes, cold sliced ham . . ."

"As for me." Carlo let out a deep sigh. "I'd like a young goat roasted on a spit, the way we used to have it at the festival of Christmas. And a mound of spaghetti with a sauce of melted cheese . . ."

"And for dessert," continued Jeannot, as though Carlo had not interrupted with his tantalizing flashback to his mother's Italian cooking, "apple tarts, very golden and crisp, a mocha cake, some cream puffs . . ."

"Stop it, my friends," cried Paul, putting his hands over his ears. "If we eat now, I shall have no appetite for my supper of dry bread and boiled potatoes."

"That's a curious thing now," exclaimed Roland. "Dry bread and potatoes, you say. Exactly what we are planning for this evening's menu."

"Why so are we!" announced Gaston and Carlo, as though overwhelmed at this remarkable coincidence.

"Nothing so ordinary as potatoes in our household," said Jeannot, only half mockingly. "We sup on rutabaga. Every evening, rutabaga. What a flavor. What a tempting smell!" He clasped his nose in thumb and forefinger, and made a face.

"Never mind." Paul put his arm over the younger boy's shoulders. "One of these days we'll have real feasts again. Just as soon as we chase the Boches back over the Rhine."

"Every time fear grips me, I think of rutabaga," muttered Jeannot, partly to himself. It was a curious remark but Paul gave it no thought at the time.

"Here's where we leave you." Carlo and Gaston stopped short at a fork in the road at the outskirts of the town of Moyelle. "See you tomorrow." Since both of their fathers were railroad men, they lived in the Cité des Cheminots, a section of pretty stucco houses built by the railroads for their employees.

Paul, Roland and Jeannot, who were all sons of miners, headed for the Corons, the long narrow streets of quite dismal soot-stained brick houses, each identical to the next, which the mining company had constructed for their workers. Paul had the farthest to go.

"So long, Roland and Jeannot. See you soon."

"So long, Paul." Their voices echoed after him.

The afternoon of sport had exhilarated Paul and he whistled as he strode along toward his home. It was nearly seven, the hour of curfew—another German innovation—and he hastened his steps. Suddenly a shadowy form loomed ahead of him in the approaching dusk. For a moment his muscles tensed. Then he relaxed. It was only Robert, a grizzled old man with old-fashioned handlebar mustaches, the poor simple-minded brother of Mademoiselle Ricard, Paul's English teacher.

"*Bonjour,* Monsieur Robert," he said kindly. "How's everything with you?"

The old man drew himself to a halt, his eyes filled with a secret fear.

"They are after me," he muttered. "Soon it will be too late."

"Everything's all right now, monsieur," Paul reassured him. "Nobody is going to hurt you."

Old Robert shook his head and lurched past Paul, mumbling to himself. The youth looked after him thoughtfully. As long as he could remember, the old man had wandered around town greeting everyone with those sinister words, "Soon it will be too late."

No one laughed at him. All knew his story. In 1906, ten-year-old Robert Ricard had been working in the mines at Courrières at the time of the terrible catastrophe which took two thousand lives. With a dozen other miners, the boy had been trapped for twenty days in a mine gallery, most of the time without light, food and water. One by one they had perished, until only Robert was left. For months after his rescue he had not spoken. "Soon it will be too late," was the first thing he said when he regained his voice. It was almost the only thing he had ever said since then.

Today it seemed to Paul that the familiar sentence had an ominous meaning and he shivered with a curious presentiment of disaster. Yet disaster had been their way of life ever since the radio first released the news that the Maginot Line had not stopped the German tanks.

A German detachment was stationed in Moyelle, requisitioning for their headquarters a women's store with the frivolous name of Frou Frou. There had been something unreal about their presence at first. Even the stout, red-faced Kommandant Schmidt, who was in charge of the garrison at Moyelle, was like a comedy character in a play. At an open meeting in the town square the Kommandant in his ridiculous broken French proclaimed that the Germans were here as their friends and as their liberators. They had nothing to fear, he assured them, so long as they observed law and order.

Whose law and order? The people of Moyelle soon found out.

A new way of life began. Almost overnight the shelves of the grocery stores were empty. Those first weeks one had to stand in line all day for a loaf of bread. Butter and meat vanished. Later strict food rationing was established but even so there was not enough for everyone.

Women who had no milk for their babies marched to the Town Hall, carrying black flags and calling themselves the Parade of Famine. They asked to see the Mayor but it was the Chief of Police who appeared to speak to them. He had already decided to butter his bread with the Nazis and told them patronizingly that he regretted as much as they the lack of milk.

"And why then do you with no small children get two quarts each morning?" cried out one of the women, who had talked with his servant.

The others set on him with the staffs of their flags, beating him over the head and shoulders until the French gendarmes pulled them off. But nobody was arrested. Not then.

The morning of Armistice Day, November 11, six months after the German invasion, dozens of little paper tricolor flags appeared on walls, fences, even pasted on the windowpanes of Frou Frou's, the Nazi headquarters, and on top of a high-tension pole, a full-sized French flag waved gloriously. The town's power had to be turned off before a German soldier could scale the pole and bring it down, with Kommandant Schmidt barking angry orders from the ground.

Paul had no idea who was responsible for the appearance of the flags, and no one else seemed to know either. But all that day the people of Moyelle had a cheerful look, for the first time since the occupation.

The mines were now under German control. The coal which should have gone to warm French homes and run French factories was being shipped into Germany.

"It is shameful," Paul's father, Jules La Coque, said once at supper. "It is shameful and it is unbearable."

Frequently some of his comrades from the mines dropped in, and the men sat around the kitchen, talking in low voices. In spite of the curfew, Monsieur La Coque sometimes stayed away until very late, giving no reason for his absences. When Paul once asked him where he had been, he merely shrugged his shoulders.

"These days, my son," he said quietly, "it is wise to hear nothing, see nothing, and say nothing."

One night it was nearly dawn when Paul heard him climbing the stairs to his bedroom. The next morning, when Paul was in the cellar filling the coal scuttle, he found a leaflet apparently pushed through the coal shaft. It announced that beginning that day all the miners were on strike.

Excitedly he took it to his father.

"Well now," Monsieur La Coque said, smiling. "Isn't that splendid? I'll have a few days to rest up."

Paul suspected that his father already knew about the strike, but he had now learned to repress his curiosity.

The miners continued on strike all week. Unlike ordinary strikes, there were no meetings, pickets or parades. All that happened was that the men stayed home. Eight days after it started, German trucks roared up and down the empty Corons, blaring out on loudspeakers the good news that the miners would, if they returned to work, receive increased rations in bread, butter, meat, soap and tobacco.

Monsieur Michel, Roland's father, a thickset robust man with mighty shoulders, stopped by the La Coque house that afternoon. Madame La Coque brought up a bottle of good wine from the cellar and poured the two men a drink.

"To a great victory," said Monsieur Michel jubilantly, raising his glass. "To the first open resistance in France since the Germans came! We have reason to celebrate."

Paul's father raised his glass too but his face was somber. "It is a victory," he agreed, "but it is too soon to rejoice. We must not deceive ourselves. The matter is not closed. The Nazis are not going to forget or forgive that no Pas de Calais miner dug a single lump of coal for them during an entire week."

This was the first time Paul had known that miners in neighboring communities had been on strike too.

All these recent events were flashing through his mind when he rounded the corner of his own street, the Rue de la Bastille—and saw a truck blocking the road, with its headlights shining directly on the front door of his house! Several soldiers were standing by it. By their dark uniforms, military caps and broad shiny belts, he knew they were the Gestapo. The Gestapo, the dread Nazi secret police, were stationed in Lille, fifty miles away, and rarely appeared in Moyelle. Paul felt as though he had been kicked in the pit of the stomach.

He started running toward his home but slowed down cautiously as the front door opened. Out walked his father, dressed in his work clothes, leather jacket and beret, holding himself tall and proud and with the habitual dignity that made all others in Paul's eyes seem lesser men. His expression was stern and slightly contemptuous. A Gestapo soldier was on each side of him. Madame La Coque followed them out, with eight-year-old Emile at her side and little Mitzi clinging to her apron.

Trust his mother not to be afraid, even of the Gestapo.

"You swine!" she shouted. "How dare you break into our house with your dirty boots! My husband is an honorable man. He has never done anything wrong in his life."

"Hold your tongue, madame," said one of the Gestapo, apparently the officer in charge. "If you don't, we'll take you too."

"Why don't you?" she demanded, her eyes burning darkly. "It takes courage to arrest a woman, doesn't it?"

"Be quiet, Annette," Paul's father said calmly. "It's a waste of breath to talk now. Our time will come."

"Don't be insolent, La Coque," barked the officer and without warning he hit Paul's father across the face.

A wave of fury swept over Paul and he dashed up to the officer, his fists clenched. "You have no right!" he shouted wildly. "You have no right to touch my father!"

The officer, a tall thin man with a dark evil face, looked down at him indifferently. "And who is this brat?" he asked in flawless French.

"Go into the house, my son," his father said firmly. "These *gentlemen*"—he emphasized the word "gentlemen" with a tinge of sarcasm—"have promised me that they'll let me come home for supper."

In his heart, Paul knew that it was not true. The Gestapo had not come all that distance to release his father in time for supper.

"Come on. Get going." The soldiers shoved him toward the truck.

The whole scene seemed incredible. Yet it was true—not a movie nor a bad dream from which he would soon awaken. Regardless of consequences, Paul threw his arms around his father's neck, holding him tightly. "Don't go, Father. I'll not let you go."

"That's enough," snapped the officer.

The two soldiers seized Paul's wrists to break his hold and flung him to the ground. Then they forced his father into the truck and the motor started.

Paul leaped to his feet and ran after it. He had to do something, however futile. "Don't worry, Father," he called at the top of his lungs. "I'll take care of things. Everything will be all right."

When the truck was out of sight, he walked slowly back through the narrow passage between their house and the next one and in through the rear door leading into the kitchen. It was a cheerful room with wallpaper patterned in bright red flowers and a fire glowing in the coal stove. His mother, her face white and strained, was sitting in a chair next to the kitchen table, her arms around the children, the weeping Mitzi and Emile, who was valiantly trying to suppress his own sobs.

It suddenly occurred to Paul that he was now the head of the household.

"Come now," he said, placing firm hands on the heads of both children. "Father would not want you to cry. We have to manage until he comes back. We have to make him proud of us."

CHAPTER 2

FIRST MISSION

Paul did not even try to sleep that night. His brave words to his mother and the children had stilled only temporarily his own horror at the blow that had befallen them. What would the Gestapo do to his father? He did not dare think about it. Lying very still so as not to disturb little Emile at his side, he clenched his fists, as if that gesture would help to steel him against his fears.

Why had they taken his father? He guessed it had to do with the strike, that Jules La Coque was suspected of being one of the organizers. Was that all? Sabotage perhaps on those many nights when he had stayed out late? The Germans had recently plastered up posters saying that sabotage was being done by "foreign terrorists" who would be duly punished. That was silly. There were no "foreign terrorists" in Moyelle except the Nazis, and anyway who but the French would risk their safety to make things uncomfortable for the invaders? The Nazi propaganda made no sense to Paul; he doubted if they believed it themselves.

For whatever reason his father had been arrested, Paul knew it was nothing to be ashamed of. Only men of courage would willingly incur the wrath of the Germans. And now, because of his courage, he was a prisoner. This fact, which no wishful thinking would change, was like a hammer delivering repeated blows on his consciousness.

To escape from his gnawing anxiety, he forced himself to think on practical matters. "To live you must eat; to eat you must work." That was the maxim of the mining country. Paul had heard it all his life. With the breadwinner of their family gone, it would now be his job to take care of his mother and the little ones.

Many sons of miners went to work at twelve, the minimum age level for child labor, according to French law. Jeannot, for example, had started working in the mines on his twelfth birthday, several months before. Carlo and Gaston were beginning their apprenticeships for the railroad, earning a small sum as they learned their trade. Of the five close friends, only Paul and Roland were still in school.

Paul's father was determined that his children should have a good education. Education was the right of all, he said, of rich and poor alike. He felt all the more strongly about this because his own schooling had ended at the age of seven, during the First World War when Moyelle had become a battlefield and all the civilian population had to be evacuated; some, like the La Coque family, to Belgium, and others to safer parts of France. Later he had tried to make up for what he had lost, reading books he borrowed from somewhere or other on history, economics, politics, even mining engineering. It was in fact said among the other miners that Jules La Coque knew more about mining than the Engineer himself.

The Engineer, whose name was Monsieur Beaulieu, was the head of the Moyelle Mines. To be Engineer, one had to go to the University. No simple miner like Paul's father, no matter how much he learned through books or practical experience, could achieve such a position. Before the war, the Engineer was responsible only to the Board of Directors, but now of course he took orders from the Germans. No matter. Tomorrow, Paul resolved, he would get his mother's consent to ask Monsieur Beaulieu for a job.

Wide-awake still, his mind jumping from one subject to another like a grasshopper, Paul became aware of a slight sound not unlike the scratching of a pen. Instantly alert, he switched from the inner world of his thoughts to the world beyond them. The scratching sound was repeated, once, twice, and then, like a faraway phantom call he heard someone whisper "Paul." The scratching sound must be caused by pebbles thrown against his window. Someone was trying to wake him!

There were two bedrooms on the second floor of the La Coque house. His mother had taken Mitzi with her in the big bed in the front room. The small room where Paul and Emile slept was in the back, overlooking their vegetable garden. Paul listened briefly to his young brother's quiet, regular breathing, then slipped out of bed and went to the window. At first he saw nothing but the bleak silhouettes of the houses opposite.

"Paul!" The voice came as a hoarse whisper. A small figure was standing in the court, almost directly beneath him. "It's I, Jeannot. Come down. I must talk with you."

What could little Jeannot want—and at this hour?

Mystified, Paul pulled on his trousers and a jacket, and holding his shoes in his hand, tiptoed out into the hall. Was his mother sleeping? Somehow he doubted it and his suspicions were confirmed by the sound of muffled sobbing coming from her room. She had not cried before the Ge-

stapo nor in the presence of her children, but the tears she
had restrained were flowing freely now. Maybe it was better that way. At least, she was less likely to hear him should
the stairs creak.

The wooden stairway creaked easily and Paul, who usually bounded down the stairs like an elephant, as his
mother said, descended with as much stealth as he could
muster. The tiled floor of the kitchen was firm beneath his
footsteps, and then he had only to unbolt the kitchen door
and shove it open to join Jeannot.

"What . . ." he started to ask.

Jeannot, silencing him with a look, took him by the arm
and walked with him to the far end of the garden, where
they sat down on the ground beneath a dwarfed and scrag-
gly crab apple tree.

"We can talk here without being overheard," Jeannot
said softly. "You are surprised, I know, and there is very
little time to explain. We need your help tonight."

"We?" Why should Jeannot's family need him tonight?
Was someone sick? But if that were the case, why all the
aura of secrecy? Paul knew well that they were hard up,
much more so than his other friends. Monsieur Du Bois,
Jeannot's father, had lost an arm in a mine accident, and
was now employed as a watchman in the shower room at
about half the pay of a miner who dug coal. Jeannot's
fourteen-year-old sister, Lucette, worked in a silk factory
in Roubaix, a two-hour bus ride from Moyelle, earning
even less than Jeannot in the mines. The combined salaries
of the three working members of the family provided only
the barest necessities.

"I'll be glad to do anything I can to help you, Jeannot,"
Paul said aloud. "You know that."

"It's not for myself." Jeannot spoke quickly and indig-

nantly. "It's for us. I mean it's for the men who are band-
ing together to fight the Germans. The Patriots. Men like
your father."

Paul could only stare at his small friend in utter amazement.

"I'm sorry about your father, Paul." Jeannot let his hand
rest on Paul's arm in sympathy. "He was our chief. I wish
I could tell you in what esteem the men hold him. But
that's not the point now. Whatever happens to any one of
us, the others must continue. You can understand that,
can't you?"

Paul's mind was in a turmoil. Up until now, he had always been considered the leader of the five friends, and
Jeannot had accepted this leadership unquestioningly.
Now it turned out that certain older men, including his
own father, had entrusted Jeannot with matters of which
he, Paul, was in complete ignorance!

"Don't think your father lacked confidence in you,"
Jeannot was saying, as though he had read Paul's thoughts.
"He simply felt it wiser to keep you out of it until there was
a specific job for you to do. There is now. He was going
to tell you about it this evening. Now it is I who must do
so. In this work, you have to be flexible. You must adjust
your plans to the vicissitudes of circumstances."

Adjust your plans to the vicissitudes of circumstances!
What impressive language to come from little Jeannot!

"You are curious to know who are the members of the
group," he continued in this curious adult manner. "That
I cannot tell you. I myself know only two of them—my
father and one other. It is better that way. We may all feel
that we would rather die than betray a comrade but the
Nazis have ways of making people talk—even the strongest
of them."

"I would not talk," Paul muttered gruffly. He was torn between admiration and jealousy. If only he could have heard these things from his father, how proud he would have felt! But then nobody could have foreseen that Jules La Coque would be arrested that very night. It was, as Jeannot said, "the vicissitudes of circumstances."

"I don't think you would talk, Paul," Jeannot answered him gravely. "The point is we cannot afford to take chances."

"So what do you want me to do? Or can't you even tell me that?" With difficulty, Paul repressed a note of surliness from his voice.

"Naturally I can tell you," Jeannot said with a slight smile. "You know, don't you, that the Germans ship carloads of coal into Germany regularly. We can't refuse to mine that coal or we would starve. But we can on occasion keep some of it from reaching its destination. The trains go at night on the theory that nobody will know about them. One of them is leaving in about an hour. It won't go far. There's going to be an accident about a mile out of town."

"And I am to help with this—accident?" Paul demanded, suddenly quite excited.

"You won't have much sleep tonight, and tomorrow you must get up as usual," Jeannot told him. "And there's danger in it."

"What do I care about that?" Paul scowled. "Do you think I'm a coward?"

"I know you're not or I wouldn't be here," Jeannot said. "But we never force anyone to join us. It's something every man must decide for himself."

The way he said "man" appeased Paul's hurt ego and his resentment against Jeannot vanished.

"You're a good boy, little Jeannot," he murmured. "The brainiest of us all. Now tell me what my part is."

"I'll let you know all about it on the way." Jeannot pulled off his shoes. "We're better off barefoot until we get out of town, what with the curfew. Until then, not a word."

They retraced their steps through the garden, skirted along the passageway between the houses and out onto the dark street. Single file and silently they followed the narrow sidewalk. Once they heard low voices and the crunching of approaching footsteps. Slipping between two houses, they flattened themselves against the wall, scarcely breathing. The footsteps passed, and when all was quiet again, they continued.

Had they heard some Germans on night patrol or others on a secret mission like themselves? There was no way of knowing.

At last they crossed the south edge of town and were out on the open road. To their right loomed the pit heaps, great symmetrical man-made hills outlined against the starlit sky. Ahead of them stretched the fields of Vimy, still gutted with shell holes from the First World War. The air was surprisingly warm for September.

"We're safe for the moment." Jeannot breathed deeply. "Now we can put on our shoes." As he was tying his laces, he looked up at Paul and smiled. "You see, if you take each thing as it comes, you don't have time to be afraid of what comes next."

"And what does come next?" Paul demanded, consumed with curiosity.

"Our job is to act as decoys," Jeannot explained, as they resumed their trek. "We have certain advantages over grown men. We're small, comparatively so at least, can hide easily and run fast. On the nights the coal trains leave, the tracks are patrolled by guards, one every few hundred yards or so. We must keep the guard busy, so that the men will have time to lay the dynamite without being disturbed." He went on to describe how they would keep the guard busy.

"It sounds like fun," Paul commented.

"That depends." Jeannot shrugged. "Some of the guards are retired French railroad men, old fellows who do it just for the few pennies it brings them. But sometimes German soldiers serve as guards, and they carry guns. Just remember this. If you hear shooting, don't stay around. Get back to the road as fast as you can. You can understand why."

"Naturally," said Paul, with more nonchalance than he felt.

They were passing through a field, some distance from the widely separated farmhouses, when Jeannot stopped. "We'd better separate here. I'll cut off to the woods. Follow me in about three minutes. Agreed?"

"Agreed, my lieutenant." Paul raised his arm in a mock salute, adding, "Okay, pal," an expression he had heard in the American movies.

Impulsively Jeannot reached out to shake his hand. "Good luck," he whispered. "And be careful." He turned and scampered off in the darkness.

Alone, Paul stood gazing at the skies. The clouds, never far away in "the black country," had returned to hide the stars. The night, serene and mysterious, was guarding her secrets. Many times in broad daylight he and the other boys had explored this countryside, searching for shells or other souvenirs of the bloody battles of the First World War which had been fought here.

How different it was at night! Why should he suddenly

feel cold? Was it fear? He refused to admit it, even to himself. He was not going to disgrace himself before Jeannot, a year younger than himself. He must be worthy of his father. From the skies, it seemed to him the muted word "Courage!" floated down. The old women of Moyelle often said that the road between their town and Vimy was haunted by the spirits of the soldiers who had died there. If so, these same soldiers were now calling on him to continue their fight.

By now Jeannot had had enough time for a head start. Paul straightened his shoulders, pressed his lips together as his father did when there was work to do, and headed across the fields toward the woods.

The woods belonged to the railroad company and lined the tracks about a hundred feet deep on each side. Before the war, Paul's family and other people of Moyelle often picnicked in this pleasant spot. Now the Germans had surrounded the wooded area with a barbed-wire fence and posted NO TRESPASSING signs at regular intervals. That the invaders had taken away the only picnic grounds in their bleak country was one more grievance, to add to all the others.

Paul reached the hated barbed wire, slithered and wiggled beneath it, proceeded on through the woods to the small slope leading up to the railroad tracks. Then he waited. Presently he heard the patrol guard approaching. He was singing to himself, a sentimental German tune, either a lullaby or a love song, Paul judged. He could be sure now that the guard was not a Frenchman! He passed so close that if Paul had had a lasso he could have swung it around his neck. When the guard had gone on some twenty-five feet, Paul purposely kicked up some loose dirt.

The singing stopped, and Paul could almost feel the guard stop, look and listen. He kicked some more dirt.

"Halt!" the guard shouted. "Who is there?"

Paul ran, noisily, down the track. The guard lumbered after him, mumbling curses. Paul darted into the woods, only now he moved stealthily. In this same spot, as a child, he had played Indian with the other boys, learning to sneak up on each other so that not even a twig cracking beneath their feet gave them away. It had been a game then but now this early training proved invaluable. He kept going until he reached a large boulder, crouching down behind it.

Nearby he could hear the guard stamping around, muttering to himself. Paul had the advantage that the guard did not know where he was, but still there were moments when his adversary was too close for comfort.

"*Ach,* you, show yourself or I'll shoot."

It sounded funny in the guard's accent, but coming almost in Paul's ear he had no desire to laugh. Just then there was a crash, as if someone had jumped from a tree into a heap of brush, and it came from the other side of the tracks. Jeannot was on the job!

"There you are!" shouted the guard, dashing off.

Paul could relax now. He rose and leaned against his boulder while Jeannot, as he had been doing, made a great deal of noise in one spot and then slipped off quietly somewhere else, leaving the guard bewildered and frustrated.

"*Ach Himmel!*" he roared. "Are you man or beast?"

It was Paul's turn, and he ran a few yards, picked up a rock, aiming it at the tracks where it made a zinging sound. Then, as the guard came storming back in his direction, he retreated swiftly to the boulder.

A little too swiftly. As he landed with a leap on the turf and underbrush, he heard something crack, the ground be-

neath him gave way, and with a crash he fell into a pit about four feet deep.

The noise alerted the guard, who came raging toward him. Paul crouched down, panic-stricken. If the German found him, he would have to fight, that was all there was to it, and he knew in advance that a thirteen-year-old boy would have a very slim chance against one of Hitler's well-trained "supermen."

Then from out of the night came a shrill, piercing screech, *"Ya-ee . . . ya-ee . . . ya-ee . . ."* It sounded like the wail of some unearthly monster, but Paul recognized it as Jeannot's own childhood version of an Indian war whoop.

"You devil!" yelled the guard. There was a series of blasts as he fired, once, twice, three times in all. As the shots died out, Paul heard the rumbling of the approaching train.

He held his breath. This was the moment. His and Jeannot's job was over. If everything worked on schedule . . . Before he could finish the thought the explosion came. There were no "ifs." An unfamiliar exultation swept over him. He was part of an anonymous group which Jeannot had referred to as "we"! Tonight, he and these unknown others had carried out a successful action against the enemy!

He knew it was safe to climb out now but he was curious about the trap into which he had fallen, and felt around in the darkness to determine the nature of the place. It was, he discovered, a rectangular dugout no more than a couple of feet wide and about three feet long, and he guessed that it dated from the First World War. Three sides were of cement but the fourth seemed to lead into a tunnel. Boards covered it on the top except for the place where he had crashed through.

How was it that nobody had ever fallen into it before? There seemed no reasonable explanation except that the wood was still in good condition in the days when picnickers and their children had swarmed over the area on their holidays. Another time he could return and explore it further. He hoisted himself up and, as an afterthought, before he left he pulled the boards back in place and covered them with an armful of underbrush. All this took but a few minutes.

"If you hear shooting, don't stay around," Jeannot had said. But Paul still hesitated to leave. What if one of those three shots had found its mark? What if Jeannot was lying helpless and wounded on the other side of the tracks? If he left without being sure Jeannot was safe, he would never forgive himself. For some twenty minutes he scouted around, calling softly, "Jeannot! Jeannot!"

There was no answer—only the engulfing blackness of night, and far down the tracks, in the direction of the explosion, guttural shouts. He had to give up his vain search, go back through the woods, under the barbed-wire fence, and across the fields to the road.

"It's about time, Paul."

Jeannot was there ahead of him, unhurt and triumphant.

"Jeannot! Are you all right?"

"You can see for yourself that I am. What took you so long?"

"I was afraid you might have been hit," Paul admitted, a little sheepishly. "I went looking for you."

Jeannot grinned. "The guard was much too upset to shoot straight. It was quite by accident, I'm sure, that the third shot went just over my head."

They exchanged experiences as they walked back to town.

"You did very well for the first time," Jeannot commented, speaking man-to-man and without patronage. "There were just two mistakes. You should not have fallen into the pit. A Patriot must learn never to miss his footing. And you shouldn't have looked for me. You should have come straight back to the road."

"I'm sorry," Paul said humbly.

"Never mind." Jeannot gave him a comradely squeeze on the arm. "All of us make mistakes. The important thing is that we learn by them—and learn fast."

"I'll do better next time."

"We did our job," Jeannot assured him. "That's what matters. And there's going to be one more trainload of French coal that does not reach a German factory or ammunition plant."

Later Paul was glad that Jeannot, in this proud moment, did not yet know the cost of that trainload of coal.

CHAPTER **3**

A BRAVE FAREWELL

The sky was growing bright when Paul tiptoed into his house and up the stairs. As he fumbled for the doorknob to his room, he heard his mother's voice:

"Paul!"

He kept quiet, hoping she would decide she had imagined hearing him. But trust his mother's ears—or instinct.

"I know you're there, Paul. Come in."

"Yes, Mother." Obediently he went into her room and approached her bedside. He could barely see the outlines of his mother's face and the bundle of bedclothes at her side which was little Mitzi.

"Are you all right?" Her voice was low, but cross with anxiety.

"Yes, Mother." He felt strangely like a little boy waiting for a scolding.

"Where have you been?"

"Out in the garden. I couldn't sleep." That was the truth as far as it went.

"You're not telling me everything."

"No, Mother. I can't." He reached over and stroked her hair.

She pushed his hand away. "Don't tell me you're going to start the same business as your father. I cannot endure it."

"I'm sorry." He did not succeed in sounding repentant.

"It's not fair! You're only a child. There are men to do that sort of thing. I won't permit it."

Madame La Coque was not a modern woman, not the sort who crusades for the right of women to vote and for their equality with men. She did not, like her husband, read books on politics and history. Her role was to run the household, and all of her household duties she performed superbly well—cooking, sewing, washing, ironing, cleaning. Within her own home she was Queen. They all depended on her and they all obeyed her. Paul could not go against her wishes, but he had to make her understand how important it was that he continue what his father had started.

"We French cannot live as slaves, Mother," he said gently. "That's what the Nazis want us to do. We must fight them—in every way we can—every one of us."

Her mother stared up at him, her dark eyes sad and thoughtful. "You're just like your father," she said unexpectedly. "Your hair is brown and wavy like his and you have the same determined chin. When you make up your mind, there's no changing it. All right, do what you have to do, I won't interfere. Only be careful." Then she turned over, averting her face from his.

The bundle of bedclothes beside her moved. "Mama!" cried little Mitzi sleepily. "What's the matter, Mama? Hold me."

"There, there, my chicken. Everything's all right." She put her arms around the child and held her tightly, not even seeming to notice when Paul left the room.

Once in bed again, he fell asleep almost immediately,

and although he had fully intended to be the first one up, he was awakened only by Emile tugging at him.

"Get up, Paul. Hurry. We're going to see Papa."

"Father! Is he here?" Paul was already half out of bed.

"Not here. At the *gendarmerie*. The police station. A man stopped by and told us. He said we should go there at once."

Paul was dressed and downstairs in the space of a few seconds. The fire was burning in the stove and his mother had poured him a cup of the weak brew of chicory which passed for coffee now. She was slicing the rest of their bread, spreading it thickly with their entire week's butter ration. Her motions were rapid and nervous.

"Drink your coffee, Paul. I'm making sandwiches for your father and taking him some socks and a clean shirt."

A few moments later the mother and her three offspring were trudging the Coron streets toward the police station. The skies were cloudy and it was misting. Paul felt numb and weary from his sleepless night, but his steps were firm. Emile looked grave and tense. All were silent except for little Mitzi, who took this occasion to prattle on in her childish fashion.

"We're going to see Papa. He is going away. I don't want him to go. I want him to come home with us. I will tell him to come home. I will tell him that pretty soon Père Noël will be here and bring us peppermint sticks and cookies."

Paul glanced at his mother. She was a slender woman with high cheekbones and dark hair, which she combed smoothly into a coil at the back of her neck. For this occasion she had put on her best suit, the one she wore on Sundays, and she was wearing the high-heeled pumps which her husband had bought her before the war, walking gingerly in them along the muddy road. She was extremely pale.

"You look pretty, Mother. He will be glad to see you looking so nice." Paul stooped down and picked up his baby sister in his arms.

"Ride piggyback, Mitzi?"

"Yes, yes," she squealed delightedly.

"Up you go." He swung her high over his shoulders, letting her clasp her plump legs around his neck.

"Play horse!" she cried. "Paul play horse with Mitzi. Get-up, get-up, Mitzi's horse!"

And so they cantered along until they got in sight of the *gendarmerie,* a big brick building with barred windows, when Paul gently set her down.

There were other women and children in front of the building, some weeping, some quiet with fear in their eyes, some talking angrily. Two French gendarmes—policemen— were standing guard at the entrance, and there was a big empty truck on the street.

Madame La Coque, holding Mitzi's hand tight, approached one of the gendarmes.

"Monsieur," she said. "I'm looking for my husband. Can you tell me if he is here? He is called Jules La Coque."

The gendarme looked down at her and said not unpolitely, "I know nothing, madame."

"Please," she pleaded. "I must find him. I have a package for him."

"Was he one of those arrested last night for activities against the government?" asked the gendarme.

Paul saw his mother flush. "He was an honest man, monsieur. He wouldn't do anything wrong."

"If your husband was arrested, madame, it was because

he broke the law," the gendarme insisted. "You should know that laws are made to be obeyed."

Paul half expected his mother to burst out in a tirade against this traitor but instead she replied meekly. "All my husband wanted, monsieur, was that France should be free again. You are a Frenchman too. Surely you won't condemn him."

The gendarme had the grace to look uncomfortable. "I am not a judge, madame. I can't condemn anybody. I have my own job to do."

In spite of his better judgment, Paul burst out, "It's not the job of a Frenchman to take orders from the Boches."

"Paul, be quiet." His mother turned to the gendarme. "Please forgive my son. He is upset. A good boy but speaks without thinking. Perhaps you have a son of your own, monsieur. If you were called away, you too would want to see him before you left."

The gendarme relented a little. "The men brought in last night slept in the basement here," he told them. "If you will wait patiently, madame, perhaps you will see them. Your husband may be among them."

"Thank you, monsieur."

As they joined the other waiting families, one of the women addressed Paul's mother. "Have you heard the news, madame? It is all because of the train wreck last night."

"What train wreck?" Madame La Coque asked.

"They say it was dynamite," the woman confided. "Ten carloads of coal were overturned. The locomotive was wrecked and the driver was killed."

"A Frenchman?"

"Ah no." The other, a sharp-featured angular woman with a man's sweater pulled over her long black dress, shook her head. "Unfortunately, it was a German. Otherwise, perhaps our husbands would have been released. Or at least held in a French prison. As it is they have all been made hostages and are to be deported out of the country. My own husband is among them and I can tell you I do not feel very friendly toward the men who did that sabotage. . . ."

So this was the penalty! So this was the Nazi method! To punish prisoners they already held for deeds done by others. Paul felt himself seized by impotent rage.

At that moment the *gendarmerie* door opened and out came the Moyelle Chief of Police, accompanied by Kommandant Schmidt. They were followed by about a dozen prisoners, handcuffed two by two and escorted by German soldiers. Jules La Coque, pale and unshaven, but holding his head high, was among them, handcuffed to Monsieur Michel. Orders were shouted in German; the men were brought to a halt before the truck.

Roland was in the same situation then that he was! That was Paul's first thought.

The La Coque and Michel families had been close since the two boys were babies. In happier times they usually had Sunday dinners together. After they had eaten, Monsieur Michel played his accordion and they all sang. Whereas Paul's father was by nature serious and a little withdrawn, André Michel was just the opposite, full of fun, with a way of telling stories that would bring tears of laughter to their eyes. The two men were inseparable, and Paul and Roland, who was an only son, had grown up like brothers. Paul was quicker in his studies, especially in history, but Roland excelled in manual training or any work where he could use his hands.

An argument started between the French Chief of Police

and the German Kommandant. As far as Paul could judge, the Kommandant was bawling out the Chief of Police for something or other; the latter, red-faced and stammering, seemed to be attempting to justify or defend himself. Women and children seized this opportunity to cluster around the prisoners. Paul dashed up to his father.

"We brought you some bread, Father." There were many more important matters to discuss but this was the first thing that came into his head.

"Splendid." His father smiled down at him. "I appreciate that. Last night I seemed to have missed my supper." He took the package which his wife thrust into his free hand.

"There are some clean socks," she said. "Mind you take care of yourself, Jules. You know how easily you catch cold."

"I'll do my best," he promised gravely.

"Don't worry, Annette," Monsieur Michel addressed Paul's mother. "I'll keep an eye on him. He won't be able to get very far from me." Mockingly, he raised his handcuffed wrist.

"Ah, yes," broke in another prisoner. "Up to this time the only chains we knew were those our wives put on us. Chains of silk, of course."

The others joined in, making wisecracks about the fix they were in, being chained to each other instead of to the women they had married.

"And my wife?" Monsieur Michel asked almost too casually. "She did not come with you? She couldn't miss her beauty sleep?"

"Lose sleep to see a rogue like you?" demanded Madame La Coque, falling into the spirit of banter. "A woman is a fool to lose sleep over any man. This afternoon I'll go have coffee with her. I'll tell her you're off to find another woman."

All the women who had looked so tearful a few moments before were now greeting their husbands with cheerful smiles, much as if they were going on a day's fishing trip instead of to an unknown fate, while the men themselves were joking and jesting with the utmost nonchalance. It was as though a conspiracy existed between them, the prisoners and their families, to put on their bravest front before those stiff German soldiers, standing with their rifles at their sides, their chins held painfully high. As though they had all talked it over in advance and decided: "The enemy is going to see what we're made of. No tears, mind you."

"Paul, my boy." His father rested his free hand on his shoulder. "I know I can count on you to take over."

"Yes, Father. You can. I will. I have already . . ." He stopped, wishing he could tell the whole story of the night before.

"I was sure of it." His father nodded. He turned to Emile. "You must grow up a little faster than I wanted you to, Emile. Be a good boy and look after your mother while I am gone."

"I will, Father," Emile promised, his chubby face serious.

"Papa," cried Mitzi at this moment. "Kiss me, Papa. Kiss Mitzi."

Then the whole family was embracing him.

A big sleek black car drove up and out of it stepped the same Gestapo officer who had arrested Jules La Coque the night before.

"What's going on here?" he barked at Kommandant Schmidt, who promptly stopped his argument with the

Chief of Police and stood at attention. "What is the meaning of this disorder? Get them into the truck. Fast."

The Chief of Police disappeared into the *gendarmerie.* The Kommandant shouted at his men. The German soldiers pushed the prisoners into the truck and climbed in after them, while the gendarmes watched, their faces expressionless. The truck started.

"Au revoir! A bientôt! We'll see you soon," called the women.

"Good-bye," shouted the men, waving. "Keep the soup on the stove. We'll be back."

Monsieur La Coque was at the rear of the truck, and he, usually so undemonstrative, was waving the hardest of all. It seemed to Paul he would always remember his father like that, so strong and confident and defiant.

As they started toward home, they were joined by the woman with whom his mother had been talking.

"It was a brave show," she said to Paul's mother, "but I'll admit frankly, madame, my heart wasn't in it. I told my husband he should be careful. I told him he should think first of me and his children. 'What are we going to do if they catch you?' I asked him. 'How are we going to get along?' But he wouldn't listen to me."

"I will be frank too, madame," said Paul's mother. "I feel you're making a mistake. Every man loves his family, but for a man with a conscience his country comes first."

The older woman bristled. "Words sound good but you can't feed your children on them, madame. Ah, if only my Jacques had listened to me! What am I to do now? I just don't know."

"It will be hard," agreed Madame La Coque, stooping to lift Mitzi over a mudhole. "The thing to remember, madame, is that they were fighting not only for us but for all the women and children of France. Bad as it is for us now, I know that if Jules were different I couldn't love him and respect him as I do."

Ordinarily Paul was bored with woman talk—dealing as it so often did with babies and yard goods and the price of potatoes—but he could not help being proud of his mother and her effort to explain the meaning of patriotism to this ignorant woman. It was in vain, however. The woman kept on her stream of complaints, uttered in a harsh high-pitched nagging voice, and Paul stopped listening until suddenly certain of her words pierced his mind like sharp needles.

". . . and that man who was killed in the explosion, he had eight children. How do you think his wife must feel? If he'd just stayed at home in bed, it never would have happened."

"Pardon, madame," Paul interrupted, "who was the man who was killed?"

"Why one of those who set the dynamite, my boy," she said. "At the last moment, I understand, he went back to check it. It exploded right in his face. His wife reached there just as he was dying—someone must have told her— but they wouldn't let her have his body."

"Do you know his name?" Paul felt a sudden cold apprehension.

"Ah, yes. What is it? He works in the shower room at the mine—the man with only one arm . . ."

That was all Paul needed to know. Jeannot's father! Murmuring some excuse to the women, he left abruptly, dashing down a side street in the direction of the Du Bois house.

In content if not in shape, the Du Bois house resembled the shoe of the old woman of Mother Goose fame. At any hour of the day, it overflowed with little ones—pouring out everywhere—all dressed in faded, much mended school aprons handed down from one to another. Even Paul had trouble keeping them straight: the baby, Raymonde; Maurice, age three; Marcelline, age four; the twins, Gilbert and Gilberte, who were six; Mark who was ten—in addition to the two oldest, Lucette and Jeannot. With a brood like that to mind, Madame Du Bois had her hands full. Usually they could be heard even before they could be seen—laughing, crying, fighting, playing—but today as Paul approached, the house looked deserted. Not even one little head popped up from around a corner.

With a newly learned caution, he slowed up his steps and walked quietly around toward the back door. In this Coron the houses were bigger than on Paul's street; by the rules of the union they were assigned to miners with large families. Each had three rooms upstairs and three downstairs, including a big kitchen with the window facing the side. They were not jammed close together, either, but had space for flower or vegetable gardens between them.

As Paul passed the kitchen window on his way to the back door, something prompted him to glance within. There, right against the pane, was a khaki-uniformed back of such massive proportions that it could belong to only one man in Moyelle—the Kommandant Schmidt. He must have come here directly from the *gendarmerie,* probably on the orders of the Gestapo officer. Paul dropped out of sight, crouching beneath the windowsill. Though he had been taught that eavesdropping was unforgivable, he now without compunction held his breath to catch every word. This was easy so far as the Kommandant was concerned; his voice was an angry shout.

"Once more, madame, I ask you. Who tell you your husband killed by dynamite?"

Then Paul heard Madame Du Bois speak clearly and quietly, as to a child. "I have told you, Monsieur le Kommandant. No one told me. I was asleep. And I had a dream. My husband appeared to me in that dream and he said, 'I am hurt, Marie-Rose.' Marie-Rose is my first name, monsieur. 'Come to me by the railroad tracks before I die,' my husband said in the dream. What could I do? I rose and dressed and ran all the way to where my husband was lying, surrounded by your men. He died in my arms. Surely your men have told you this, monsieur."

"Nonsense!" barked the Kommandant. "How you expect me to believe such imbecility! The man who came and told you—You will gif me his name."

"My husband was alone." Madame Du Bois's voice sounded tired. "No one was with him."

The Kommandant snorted. "Alone? Madame, the guard patrol has told us. There were many men—the whole length of the tracks. They jumped on him and held him until the dynamite went off. We know who they are."

No, you don't, thought Paul. The guard would not have told, even had he known, that he was off schedule because of two boys who kept their distance from him.

"If your guard knows who they are, you have no need of me," Madame Du Bois was saying.

Paul risked a glance over the windowsill. The Kommandant had moved over to the kitchen table and was pounding it with his fist. "If you won't gif me their names, I will have you arrested."

"Arrest me then," said Madame Du Bois wearily. "I can only tell you what I know. My husband came to me in a dream . . ."

"Pfaugh!" The Kommandant seemed ready to burst with rage—and suddenly it was not only against little Madame Du Bois. "This terrible country," he roared out, "with your coal dust, your old hags and your ragamuffin children. All talking in riddles! And the Colonel, he say I haf too much trouble here. As though it was my fault. You know what I was promised, madame? Paris! Yes, Paris. Champagne and beautiful women. *Ja!* And this is what they gif me."

"I am sad for you." Madame Du Bois spoke in a monotone. "Now do you want me to go with you? If you will wait a moment I will get my pocketbook."

"No!" he yelled at her. "I not want to see you again. But later you will talk. You will gif me the names."

Turning, he stalked out—through the dining room to the front entrance, luckily for Paul, since he was able to slip in the house by the back door unnoticed. He entered to hear the violent slamming of the front door, heralding the Kommandant's departure. In the kitchen the whole family was assembled, lined up as for a family photograph, Madame Du Bois, a careworn woman who looked much older than she was, seated at the table with the baby Raymonde in her arms, Jeannot, Lucette and the younger ones all grouped around her.

"Paul, you just missed the Kommandant," cried Jeannot.

"I know, I heard everything," Paul admitted. "I am sorry . . . I have come to give you my sympathy, Madame Du Bois."

"Thank you, Paul," she said, her face gray with strain.

Unable to control herself longer, she collapsed into sobs, the smaller children following suit. The baby started to howl. Lucette picked her up.

"You go to bed, Mother. I'll fix the children something to eat."

"Come, Paul." Jeannot led his friend into the dining room, the room which none of the family ever entered except for Sunday dinners or other special occasions, the room now defiled with the boots of the Kommandant.

"Your father was a fine man, Jeannot," Paul said softly. "It is not fair that this should have happened."

"My father died doing his duty." Jeannot looked stonily ahead. "It is the best way to die."

Paul put his arm around the younger boy's shoulders. "I know how you feel, little Jeannot. We'll get our revenge."

"Yes," said Jeannot, choking. "We'll not rest until they are all driven out of the country."

"We will not rest," repeated Paul, grasping his friend's hand.

It was like a solemn vow.

CHAPTER 4

TO EAT YOU MUST WORK

It was dinnertime when Paul reached home.

His mother welcomed him with a nod. "Oh, so you're back, Paul. Good."

The kitchen table was set for the four of them, one on each side. It looked forlorn. Madame La Coque usually had Mitzi sit next to her, opposite her husband.

"Sit in your father's place, Paul." She filled their plates from the kettle on the stove. Their meal was stew, made of turnips, onions from the garden, a small piece of pork fat. Paul usually raised a fuss about turnips which he detested, but today he was hardly aware what he was eating.

"What's the matter, Paul? Are you sick?" his mother asked.

"No, Mother." He toyed with his food until the children, who ate fast to get it over with, had finished and gone outside to play. The night before he had made up his mind to something. There was no use putting it off.

"Mother," he announced when they were alone, "I'm going to work in the mines."

"Ah, no," she said quickly. "Your father wouldn't want that. You're going to continue at school."

"How much money do we have?" he demanded bluntly.

"That's not your business."

"It is now."

She looked at him strangely and then sighed. "Perhaps you are right. I have only you to depend on now. If you must know, we have about two hundred francs until next Friday. Then I ought to be able to collect your father's last two weeks' pay. That should hold us for a while."

"And when that is gone?" Paul persisted.

"I'll find a job. That woman who walked home with us told me that they are hiring sugar beet pickers at twenty-five francs a day."

"Mother, you couldn't do that sort of work," Paul protested. "You're not strong enough. Have you any idea what it's like? You work from seven in the morning until seven at night. You bend over all the time and your back aches frightfully but there's nothing you can do about it. And sometimes the sun is so hot you almost faint or else it rains and you catch cold and maybe pleurisy and you have to keep on anyway. Until winter comes and you are laid off . . ." He paused, out of breath.

"How do you know so much about it?"

"Jeannot's mother tried it for a while. She told me. She's done heavy work all her life but even she had to quit." His mention of Madame Du Bois brought back to mind the tragedy that had hit Jeannot's family and he fell silent.

"I could get accustomed to it," Madame La Coque said stubbornly. "One can get accustomed to anything."

"Even if you did," Paul pointed out carefully, "the four of us could not live on twenty-five francs a day. You know that."

His mother proposed hesitantly, "If worse comes to worst we can write for help to Uncle Georges, the one who has a farm up north at Sainte-Valérie."

"You mean my great-uncle who is so closefisted he counts the matches in every matchbox to make sure he has not been cheated?"

"Paul!" she reproached him. "That's not a nice thing to say."

"It's true, isn't it?" He looked at her defiantly. "Besides, we can't take charity. Father would not want us to take charity. Not as long as I am able to work."

His mother rose and started clearing away the dishes. "I don't even want to discuss it," she said, but her voice was uncertain and Paul knew he had almost won.

"You will let me, won't you, Mother? Then you can stay home and take care of Mitzi and Emile. They need you."

"It doesn't look as if my opinion matters any more."

"That's not true. You know I can't work without your consent. I'll quit and go back to school as soon as Father comes home."

"All right," she agreed reluctantly. "If you insist, to-morrow we'll go talk to the Engineer and see what he says."

That he would be applying for his first job with his mother did not bother Paul, since that was the custom of the country. In spite of his depression he felt a certain glow. Soon, that is if the Engineer approved, he would be earning his living like a man.

His mother poured out coffee for them in tiny cups and sat down opposite him.

"I used to sit with your father like this drinking coffee after dinner when you children were off to school or out playing. That was one of the nicest moments of the day. Ah, Paul, how long do you think it will be until . . ."

Her words were interrupted by a knock on the door.

"Come in."

It was Roland and his mother. Madame Michel was a buxom red-haired woman, very handsome and, like many attractive women, rather vain. Usually she would not go out unless she had fixed her hair nicely and put on lipstick. Today her hair was in disorder and her eyes were red with weeping. Even Paul could tell that she had not given her appearance a thought.

"Oh, Annette," she burst out, "I'll never forgive myself. Why didn't someone tell me they were leaving? Why did I have to learn it from the neighbors when it was too late? André will think I was too lazy to get up. And now I may never see him again." Her voice broke off in a pathetic wail.

"Calm yourself, Mother. Of course Father is coming back. Very soon." Roland glared at Paul as though for confirmation, and then, remembering his manners, murmured, "Good day, Madame La Coque. Hello, Paul."

"Sit down, Hélène, and have a cup of coffee," Paul's mother said. "André knows very well that you would have come if you had known. I talked with him this morning and promised him I'd see you this afternoon and tell you good-bye for him. He said you must not get upset. He's not worried about himself, just about how you will manage in his absence. He said as much."

His mother was putting words into Monsieur Michel's mouth, but Paul realized that now was not the moment to describe the curious spirit of that brief and fragmentary reunion. He looked at Roland meaningfully. Leaving their mothers to console each other, the two boys slipped out into the garden, walking out to the crab apple tree where Paul had talked with Jeannot the night before. They squatted down on their heels, to discuss the events that had so changed their lives in the last twenty-four hours.

"You know what?" Paul confided. "Tomorrow I'm going to the mines and try to get a job."

"You are?" Roland pursed up his lips. "Then I'm going too. The idea had already occurred to me. Mother is so helpless, she is like a child. I'm going to have to look after her."

"Good. At least we'll be together." Paul smiled ruefully. "We won't earn much but we can keep the wolf away. Imagine! You, I and Jeannot, all miners."

"It's worse for Jeannot," Roland said. "Our fathers are coming back. At least there's every reason why they should. Jeannot doesn't have that to look forward to."

"He has a lot of courage for such a little one." Paul chewed on a blade of grass thoughtfully, wishing he dared tell Roland all he knew about Jeannot's courage.

"That goes without saying." Roland picked up a small stick and pushed it against the ground until it broke. "I don't know who betrayed our fathers and I suppose we'll never know, but I do know one thing. I want to continue whatever work they were doing. Why don't the five of us organize a group of some sort to fight the Boches? I'm sure Carlo and Gaston and Jeannot would be willing. We could find something to do even if it's only to chalk up 'V for Victory' signs on the walls."

"That's not a bad idea." Paul's heart was pounding, though he made his voice purposely casual.

"Look," continued Roland eagerly. "It's our duty. I said yesterday we shouldn't think about the Germans all the time but I was wrong. I know that now. We've got to think about them until we get rid of them."

"You don't have to convince me of that, Roland." Paul

spoke earnestly. "The thing is that we must be careful. We can't rush into anything, particularly now, since the Nazis will be watching us closely because of our fathers. Let me think about it for a while."

"All right." Roland looked only half-satisfied. "But let's don't wait too long."

"We won't." Inwardly Paul resolved to talk over Roland's idea with Jeannot at the earliest opportunity.

At nine o'clock the next morning, Paul, Roland, and their mothers were sitting on a bench outside the office of Monsieur Beaulieu, waiting for the interview which Paul both wanted and dreaded. The Engineer was late. It was nearly ten when he walked briskly in.

"*Bonjour,* mesdames. *Bonjour,* my boys. What can I do for you?"

His manner was polished and courteous. A real gentleman, Paul's mother called him. No miner had soft well-kept hands like those of the Engineer. Though he was only about thirty-five, he was rather stout and moved heavily, unlike the miners, who were lean and supple from their hard labor. There was another way Paul could tell he had never dug coal. Every miner had blue marks on his face, sometimes just faint pencil lines, evidence of small cuts in which coal dust had become permanently embedded. The Engineer's face was smooth and unmarked.

"It's about our boys we have come," he heard his mother say.

"Naturally. Naturally." The Engineer nodded. "I'll be with you in a moment."

A half hour later, Madame La Coque and Paul, whom Hélène Michel insisted must go first, were ushered into a spacious inner office. The Engineer was sitting behind a large mahogany desk.

"Have a seat, madame. And you too, my boy."

His mother accepted but Paul preferred to stand. He felt less at a disadvantage doing so.

"You want your son to work in the mines, madame?" Without waiting for her answer, he turned to Paul. "How old are you, my boy?"

"Almost fourteen," Paul said.

"He will be fourteen in December," his mother interposed. "He wanted to come here before but his father insisted he go on with his studies. But now . . . He is very smart, monsieur, passed first last June in his class."

"La Coque, Paul," said the Engineer, consulting a memorandum on his desk. "La Coque. His father is named Jules?"

"Yes, monsieur."

"Hmm." The Engineer drew his lips together. "I don't know, madame. I understand your husband is in some trouble, minor certainly, with the German police. We have to be very careful these days. How can I be sure your son will not . . . follow in the footsteps of his father?"

That is just what I intend to do, Paul said to himself.

"Paul is a good boy, monsieur. He is strong and not afraid of work. It was his idea to come here because he knows that otherwise there would be misery in our household. You need have no fear in hiring him, monsieur." His mother spoke rapidly though her eyes were downcast.

She was interrupted by the ringing of the phone on the Engineer's desk. Paul stared at it curiously. No miner's home had the luxury of a telephone. Except for the one at the post office, it was the first he had seen.

Monsieur Beaulieu picked up the receiver. "Hello. Who

is it?" he demanded brusquely. Then the tone of his voice
changed. "Ah, *bonjour*, Monsieur le Kommandant. What
can I do for you? . . . My report? Was something wrong
with it, sir? . . . Yes, I know, production is down some-
what, but then we've had an unusual amount of sickness
among the men. . . . But what can I do? If they say
they're sick and the doctor says they're sick? . . . All right,
more fines, if you say so. . . . No, I don't want to argue
about it. . . . But there's another thing. Gustave, the delegate, tells me the men are complaining about the coal dust
along the tunnels. . . . No, not because it's dirty, because
it's inflammable. I mean, if you set a match to it, or if a
spark touched it, it would go up in flames. . . . Surely
something can be done about it. We can clean it out or else
install a watering system. . . . Yes, that would be even
more expensive. . . . You may be right. Perhaps the men
do exaggerate, I can't say. . . . As you wish, Monsieur le
Kommandant. . . ."

He glanced up at his visitors, and, suddenly aware they
were listening, broke off into a few sentences in halting
German which Paul could not understand.

His face was flushed when he hung up. "You must understand, my friends, that the Germans run the mines now,"
he said to the two of them. "The Germans are an efficient
people and they like to see things run efficiently."

That was one way of putting it, but efficient or not, it
was obvious to Paul that Kommandant Schmidt knew little
about mining.

"I understand." There was an undertone of reproach in
Madame La Coque's voice. "Perhaps you are right, monsieur. Perhaps my son is too young . . ."

"Mother!" Paul protested. "I am not too young. You
should not say that."

"He has a good spirit." The Engineer smiled. "Very well. La Coque was an excellent worker, so I'm willing to give his son a try. Though if he gets out of line . . ." He threw out his hands palms up and shrugged. "If he gets out of line, there will be nothing I can do for him."

"*Bien entendu,*" said Madame La Coque, rising. "Of course, monsieur."

"Paul, report to work tomorrow morning at five. Your mother knows the clothes you will need."

"Yes, monsieur."

"And remember," the Engineer added. "It is not a picnic in the mines. You must act like a man and you'll be treated like a man."

"I'll do my best, monsieur."

As Monsieur Beaulieu rose to escort them to the door, Paul noted with some pride that they were almost the same height.

Madame Michel and Roland were summoned next. Paul and his mother waited for them outside the mine gates.

"I am not happy about this," she confessed to Paul. "Did you hear what he said to the German Kommandant? There is too much coal dust in the mine. It is dangerous."

"Why must you worry so, Mother?" Paul broke in impatiently. "Everything will be all right."

"I hope so." She smiled at him proudly. "But women are never free from worry so long as their menfolk are in the mines. It has always been like that and I think it always will be."

Shortly Roland and his mother came out of the Administration Building and joined them.

"He took me," Roland exclaimed excitedly. "I start tomorrow morning at five. At first he hesitated because Father was arrested but then he said that after all he would give me a chance."

Paul nodded somberly. "He said the same thing to me." Though he had not shared his mother's worry about the danger, his enthusiasm was definitely dampened by the concrete evidence of German control he had witnessed. That he had known this in theory before did not lessen his distaste for working for the enemy.

Back in his office, the Engineer sat alone, tapping his desk nervously. He had handled the matter well, he told himself. Boys were needed in the mines. They worked hard and cost little. Those two would surely watch their step, if only because their salaries were desperately needed at home. But somehow he felt no satisfaction about it.

Before the war he had prided himself that the miners really liked him. He had learned to speak their patois and often they would come to him with their troubles. Now they avoided him. How unfair it was! On the one hand, the Kommandant was on his neck because production was not higher; on the other, his own men cold-shouldered him. What did they expect him to do—resign his job and go off and starve? It was easy for the miners to risk their future; they had always been poor and had little to lose, he reasoned. It was different with him. He had a big house to keep up, servants, a pretty, expensive wife who never had enough Paris frocks. He simply could not afford to get himself in trouble with the Germans.

No matter how well reasoned the arguments were with which he justified his position, he was still an unhappy man.

CHAPTER *5*

THE CHAMBER OF THE UNDERGROUND

Paul and Roland were walking down the road toward Vimy, their hands in their pockets and their berets cockily on the side of their heads. The leaves of the poplar trees along the road had turned bright yellow, and though it was November and the air was crisp, the afternoon sun was shining in an all blue sky. They had finished their work in the mines for the day, showered, eaten substantially if not wholly to their taste. It was impossible not to be cheerful on such a day.

"What are you thinking, Roland?"

"Me? Nothing," said Roland. "What are you thinking about, Paul?"

"I'm thinking about what you think about when you think of nothing," Paul reeled off glibly. It was an old gag, but one they liked. "What are you thinking?"

"Me? I'm thinking of the death of Louis XIV," said Roland.

They could go on like this for hours, when they were in the mood.

"The King is dead. Long live the King," murmured Paul, apropos of nothing.

"Why?" demanded Roland. "Why, if the King is dead, does one say 'Long live the King!'? That's always bothered me."

"It has?" Paul laughed. "Nothing could be simpler. In the old days, when a king died, his son or nearest relative immediately became ruler in his place. Then people forgot about the old king and cheered the new one."

"Things are different now," commented Roland. "We don't forget about France and cry 'Long live the Nazis!' On the contrary, we say that France is sleeping and will wake. . . . Do you want to know what I was really thinking about, Paul? I was thinking it was about time we organized that group I talked to you about. So we can help France to wake again."

"I haven't forgotten," said Paul. He had in fact discussed the matter several times with Jeannot. "The only thing lacking is a safe meeting place."

He stopped in the middle of the road and looked around. It was here, six weeks before, that he and Jeannot had separated to carry out their secret mission. Then the night had been filled with mystery and terror. How different it seemed in broad daylight, how peaceful and normal! The region had been swarming with Germans following the explosion, but now the excitement had died down and there was no one in sight.

"Follow me, Roland. I want to investigate something. If anyone sees you, I'll toss you a ball and we'll pretend we're playing."

"What's this all about?" asked Roland suspiciously.

"I'll explain later. Just trust me."

Roland shrugged. "As you wish."

To Paul's relief, they met no one as they crossed the fields and climbed under the barbed-wire fence into the woods. Without too much trouble he located the boulder where he had crashed into a pit, alerting the German patrol guard.

"Ah, here we are." He leaned over to sweep aside the still-undisturbed brush, revealing the broken and jagged planks beneath it.

"A German dugout perhaps?" Roland guessed quickly.

"I think so. But when I was here before I didn't have time to find out."

Paul jumped into the pit, crouched down, and looked around. "Just as I thought," he called. "There's a tunnel. Come on down, Roland. We're going exploring."

Roland was at his side in a leap. "This is something." He let out a delighted whistle. "I had a cousin who found a World War One dugout up near Arras once. It was filled with rifles and ammunition. I had no idea there was anything like it around here. Wouldn't it be great if we could fight the Boches with their own weapons?"

"We'd better not get our hopes up," Paul advised him. He was busy rearranging the brush overhead so that if anyone came by they would suspect nothing. "Shall we go? I brought a flashlight."

The tunnel was a bare eighteen inches high but the boys had scrambled through much tighter places in their six weeks in the mines. Paul led the way, crawling on hands and knees. After about ten feet the tunnel became higher until they could stand erect.

"It seems to be widening out." Paul turned the flashlight to right and left.

"Why, it's a room!" cried Roland.

"So it is."

The flashlight now revealed a sizable chamber with solid brick walls. Along one side were several army cots covered with crumbled blankets, thick with dust. There were also several chairs and a table. On the table was a candle in a candlestick.

"Do you have a match, Roland? Maybe we can save our battery."

"I think so." Roland fumbled in his pocket. "Here you are."

Several matches went out before the wick took fire. The flame cast an eerie light over the room. The boys hardly noticed, occupied as they were in searching for treasures.

"Look here, Paul!" Roland was tugging at a heap of rubbish in a corner. "An old German helmet!" He held it up triumphantly. "My Uncle Joseph has one just like it, a souvenir of 1914 when he was fighting the Hun. See the spike at the top? It belonged to an officer."

"There's no doubt that this is a German dugout then."

They both plunged into the "rubbish heap," found more helmets, several pairs of boots with leather cracked and brittle, the rotting remains of some uniforms, and, at the very bottom, a half-dozen German Lugers!

Roland let out a shout. "Here's our arsenal!"

Paul examined one of the pistols gingerly. It was thick with rust. "I rather doubt if these will ever fire again—no matter how thoroughly we oil and polish them."

"Maybe we'll find some in better shape." Still hopeful, Roland scouted around. From under one of the cots he tugged out an old chest. "Now we'll see what we will see!"

Together they pried it open. A cloud of dust enveloped them and Paul sneezed.

"This is worse than cleaning ashes out of the stove," he groaned.

"But much more interesting." Roland pulled aside the moldy newspapers that covered the contents. Then he grimaced in disgust. "There's nothing here but tin cans."

There were dozens of the cans, all neatly packed. In the dim light, they were unable to decipher the labels nor did they much care. People of Moyelle were prejudiced against canned goods, claiming that they were the last resort of the lazy housewife.

"I don't suppose there's a chance that they might still be edible?" Paul asked. "I mean the contents, not the cans."

"Possibly. If you like things in cans." Roland shrugged disdainfully. "Besides whatever the Germans put in cans is probably garbage. They have no appreciation of good food."

"I agree with you. Still, it won't do any harm to make sure." Paul wiped off a couple of the cans with his handkerchief and thrust them inside his jacket.

From another corner, Roland dragged out an old suitcase.

"Still looking for an arsenal?" demanded Paul, grinning.

"You never can tell," Roland muttered sheepishly.

They had to break the lock on the suitcase and they opened it to find, not arms nor ammunition, but something which Paul realized might prove just as valuable—a kit of doctor's supplies. Bandages had suffered the ravages of time, but knives, scissors, scalpels, thermometers and other instruments, packed in heavy cloth, were in perfect condition.

"I think this is our clue, Roland," he said thoughtfully. "We've found an underground hospital where Germans treated their wounded. When we advanced they had to leave in a hurry, taking their patients but leaving everything else."

It was as good a solution as they were ever able to reach.

On the far side of the room hung the remnants of a tattered army blanket. Paul pushed it aside, thinking perhaps to find the closet of weapons Roland wanted so desperately. He gasped. "There's another passage here, Roland!"

Both stood and stared at the dark gaping entrance, some five feet high.

"What are we waiting for?" demanded Roland boldly. "Let's go."

"Why not?" Paul blew out the candle, turned on his flashlight, and, because after all this was his exploration party, strode ahead of Roland. He had taken only a few steps when he stumbled over something. He lowered his flashlight and his face went white. Sprawled on the earth floor was what had once been a German soldier.

For a moment the boys were speechless at this unexpected brush with death. The underground passageway suddenly seemed very sinister. The strange shadows, the murky atmosphere, and now the dead soldier all contributed to a feeling of terror. Paul's first instinct was to turn and flee, back to the pleasant countryside they had left.

"It's only a skeleton." He tried vainly to sound indifferent.

"That's all," Roland said shakily. He hesitated. "Perhaps we ought to call it quits for today. We can always come back some other time."

"Yes, we can do that."

They retraced their steps a few feet. Then Paul stopped short.

"Roland, I'm afraid," he blurted out. "Not afraid of anything in particular, just afraid. But if I leave now I'll always feel I behaved like a weakling."

Roland looked down, seemingly intent on tracing a diagram with his foot. "I guess I'm afraid too, Paul. And of what? Of shadows? Of a skeleton? It's ridiculous. The dead can't hurt us."

"Shall we continue?" asked Paul, smiling.

"Naturally. We're going to face much worse than this before the war is over. We can be sure of that. Pretend this is our first test."

With a bravado that neither felt, they turned back. And on second sight, surprisingly, the German soldier seemed a less fearsome thing. Paul in fact knelt down beside him.

"Poor fellow! What a sad way to die. I wonder if I can find out who he is."

He groped in the pockets of the old uniform and drew out a half-rotted wallet. Inside, along with some papers, was a faded photograph. He turned his flashlight on it.

"Take a look, Roland."

The photograph showed two little girls with long braids hanging over their shoulders. "His children, you suppose?" Paul replaced the photograph in the wallet and put it back where he found it, unaccountably reluctant to rob the rightful owner.

"Too bad about those little girls, waiting in vain for their father to come home," Roland said as they walked on. "Even if he was our enemy."

Paul thought of his own father and of Roland's, of whom there still was no word. Yes, it was easy to feel sympathy for these unknown children but he did not want to show it.

"It was a long time ago," he said gruffly. "They must be old women now. They must be nearly forty."

The tunnel, after the first few feet, was high and wide and in excellent condition. Paul, turning his flashlight on the walls, noticed a curious thing. While the chamber behind them had been built of modern bricks, the walls of the tunnel were made of stones, fitted together and cemented. It occurred to him that not even the methodical Germans would have found time, in the middle of a war, to construct such a solid structure. There was also, he noted, an ancient look about the passage, reminiscent of the Catacombs of Paris, which he had once visited when Jules La Coque took his family on a holiday to that most famous city.

Moyelle and its environs had known many invasions in recorded history, as Paul had often heard from his father. During which one of them was this tunnel built? Had it been constructed by the Romans who had conquered "Gaul," as France was then known, around 60 B.C.? Or at some later date by persons seeking a hiding place for themselves and their cherished possessions? Was it when the Vandals came, or the Franks who stayed to give their name to France? Or when the land was overrun by the Huns, led by their bearded and barbarian chief, Attila?

"A penny for your thoughts, Paul," Roland said.

Paul explained his theory. "If Father were here, he could probably tell when it was built."

"Suppose you're right?" Roland sounded incredulous. "What then?"

"I don't know," Paul confessed. "In normal times I suppose there'd be quite a stir about it. But these times aren't normal."

They had walked, Paul estimated, for about a mile. This might well mean they were somewhere underneath Moyelle, unless his sense of direction had failed him. The air had grown increasingly foul, and he found himself gasping and choking, as in some of the bad sections of the mine. He had been certain they would reach an exit eventually but suddenly their way was barred by a solid and heavy wooden door.

"Oh, no!" Roland shoved against it with all his strength but it did not budge. "I think I'll just collapse here. I don't have the willpower to go all the way back."

"Don't give up so easily. There's a latch." Paul had found it with his flashlight. He struggled with it and at first it seemed stuck, and then with a grinding sound the door swung open.

They were in another chamber, a small one about five feet square, also built of brick, and it was empty except for a small stool.

"What a funny smell," commented Paul, sniffing. "Almost like tobacco."

"It's just musty." Roland took the flashlight and turned it slowly from corner to corner, searching for a door. There was none.

"A dead end," said Paul, glumly. He, no more than Roland, did not relish the long hike back. Moreover, he was pressed for time.

"Maybe not." Roland had the flashlight on the ceiling. It was of cement, except in the center where there was a square of about two feet which shone dimly, like tin or some other metal. "It wouldn't be a trapdoor, would it?"

"Let's find out." Paul pressed his hands against it and to his surprise one side raised easily.

"I hear voices," he whispered.

Excitedly they listened. There was a distant murmur of which they understood nothing. Then, very distinctly, they heard footsteps. Paul lowered the trapdoor until it was almost shut, and Roland turned off the flashlight. A woman's voice reached them, clear, loud and exasperated.

"Robert, I told you to sweep out the basement yesterday. I declare you grow more helpless by the minute."

In answer came a familiar voice and familiar words. "Yes, madame. Soon it will be too late."

In the darkness Paul let out a gasp. The first voice was certainly that of Madame Josephine, the cleaning woman at the Moyelle Town Hall. For years old Robert had helped her part time, sweeping and emptying ashes. He received a small salary from the town for this work, mostly from charity. They must, therefore, be just beneath the Town Hall basement!

"You're a real problem to me since the Germans came, Robert," Madame Josephine was saying. "How they pry into everything! If they ever catch you sitting around doing nothing, they'll throw you out in a moment. . . . There, don't look so upset. You just sweep up nice and clean and nothing will happen." Her footsteps receded and almost over the boys' heads came the whisking sound of Robert's broom.

Would he ever finish? Why did he not hurry? They hardly dared breathe as they waited there in the dark—hot, dusty, and impatient. At last they heard Robert, muttering to himself, wander off. All was quiet.

Paul turned on the flashlight. "Hand me the stool, Roland. I'm going up."

"Dare we risk it?"

"We have to." With an appointment which could not wait, he had no choice.

They pushed the trapdoor up wide enough to pull themselves through, first Paul, then Roland, and found themselves in a dimly lighted storage room behind an old stove. The trapdoor fell into place with a sharp clang.

"Ouch! We should have been more careful." They waited, but apparently no one had heard. From the top, the trapdoor was simply a sheet of aluminum, the sort used to protect wooden floors against escaping sparks.

"Now what?" Roland looked at his friend.

"We've only one problem," said Paul. "To get away from here without being noticed."

The door to the storage room was not locked. They went out cautiously and made a dash down the corridor to the men's lavatory. So far so good. The lavatory was empty. As well as possible, they brushed the dust from their clothes, washed their hands and faces, combed down their hair. They sauntered out to meet Robert, resting on his broom.

"*Bonjour,* Monsieur Robert," Roland greeted him innocently. "How goes it?"

"Not good, not good." The old man looked at them with his usual blank stare. "Soon it will be too late."

"Ah no, my friend," broke in Paul, his eyes shining. "Soon it will be time. Then things will start to happen."

They left Robert and walked nonchalantly up the stairs leading to the first floor of the Town Hall. As usual at this late afternoon hour, it was filled with men and women lined up before the different clerks' windows, waiting for ration tickets or other papers. No one paid any attention to them, except for a casual greeting from some acquaintance. After all the strangeness of the last two hours, the most peculiar sensation was this return to the everyday world without incident, without anyone guessing their remarkable experience.

Once on the street again they breathed deeply of the cool autumn air.

"That," announced Roland, "was the most exciting afternoon of my life."

"Mine too," Paul agreed. He felt as exuberant as if he had been lion hunting in Africa. "You want to know what I think? The Germans found the entrance into the long tunnel after shells destroyed the old Town Hall, except for the foundations. There must have been a crash-in, and they built up the little entrance room where the stool is. They followed the passage to the far end, decided it was a good location for their hospital, and built that chamber." He chatted on, enlarging on his theories.

"I can't wait to tell people," Roland exploded happily. "Imagine their faces! That we, a couple of miners' sons— uncouth, good-for-nothing, dirty miners, as the *bourgeoisie* call us—that we should have discovered an ancient Roman aqueduct. Or something."

"Whoa there! Calm down," Paul cautioned him. "No one is to know about this."

"But why not?"

"Because," Paul informed him, "we've found the perfect meeting place for the newly formed Club of Young Patriots, of which you, I, Jeannot, Carlo and Gaston are going to be charter members. The hospital room. Our Chamber of the Underground!"

"You have it all figured out!" Roland looked his admiration.

"I have. We can't meet in our homes. We know that. We've found the perfect solution. We'll meet right under the noses of the Germans, the last place they would suspect. Of course we should not go there in the daytime again, and never all together."

"I'll talk to Gaston and Carlo tonight," Roland volunteered.

"And I'll see Jeannot." Eventually, but not yet, Roland would be told of Jeannot's relationship with the older Moyelle Patriots, but that decision was not up to Paul.

At the next corner, he stopped. "So long, Roland. I promised Mademoiselle Ricard I'd pay her a visit this afternoon. I'm already late."

"Again? You went there last week, didn't you?"

"Yes." Paul averted his eyes. "She gets pretty lonesome with only old Robert to talk with."

"I thought you said you were going to see Jeannot."

"I'll do that afterwards."

"What do you have to go see her all the time for?" Roland demanded bluntly. To him it seemed rather silly to waste time visiting with one's teacher. "Do you drink tea like an Englishman?" He held up his hand, quirking his little finger and pretending to clasp an imaginary china cup.

"She does give me tea sometimes," Paul admitted. "It's not too bad, not any worse than the coffee we drink now. But do me a favor, Roland. Don't tell any of the other boys I go there. I don't want them to think I'm teacher's pet."

"Okay," Roland agreed good-naturedly. "It's your business."

"Thanks." Paul would have liked to explain the real reason for his visits to his English teacher but that was out of the question.

Mademoiselle Ricard lived with her brother at the south end of town in a ramshackle wooden frame house, not even as comfortable as the miners' homes. Houses such as hers, known as "barracks," had been put up hastily as temporary dwellings when people started coming back to their devastated town after the First World War. The Town Council had planned to replace them with permanent houses later on, but somehow money had never been found. Though they should have been condemned, non-miners and non-railroad workers still lived in them for lack of anything better.

The schoolteacher's home was in even worse repair than most of the barracks, Paul noticed as he climbed the rickety steps and knocked on the door. Someday, he resolved, he and the other boys would come and paint it for her. Inside, however, it was cozy and pleasant, with rag rugs on the floor, several pictures on the wall, Monsieur Robert's chaise longue, several other easy chairs, and a cheery fire in the stove.

"How nice of you to come, Paul," Mademoiselle Ricard greeted him in her sprightly, rather childlike voice. "Do sit down and make yourself comfortable. I'll have a cup of tea ready in a moment."

The schoolteacher, a tiny birdlike woman, was one of the few spinsters in Moyelle. Paul had heard the gossips say that this was not for lack of opportunity but because her fiancé, an English soldier of the First World War, had died in battle. She was a favorite with the mining families because, although she was very educated, she did not put on airs or act superior, like so many of the teachers.

After she brought in the tea, Paul handed her the two cans he had taken from the Chamber of the Underground. "Would you please tell me what these are, mademoiselle?"

"Yes, certainly." She studied the labels through her spectacles. "Why, they are cans of corned beef. How wonderful!"

"Are they German, mademoiselle?"

"But no, they are American. See, the label reads, *Made in America*."

"Would they be good to eat? That is, if they were quite a few years old?"

"I should think so. You see, Paul, they pack the meat into the can steaming hot, then put the cover on quickly before any air can get in. Because there is no air, bacteria can't get in either, so the contents don't spoil. They make very good cans in America."

"Perhaps you would open one and see what it tastes like?" he suggested tentatively.

"With pleasure, Paul."

She went to the cupboard and came back with a can opener, which she deftly inserted in the rim and moved back and forth until she had cut out the round top. "I learned to do this from an English friend," she explained, half apologetically.

With a fork she sampled the contents. "It's good, Paul. You must try some."

Suspicious, he refused, but she insisted on serving him a goodly portion on a little porcelain plate. Surprisingly, he found that "corned beef" was not bad at all. Indeed, when he had cleaned up his helping, he agreed with her that the Americans made very good tin cans.

"Have some more, Paul."

"No, thank you, mademoiselle."

"Then take the rest home to your mother."

"Keep it for Monsieur Robert," he told her. "The other can is yours too. There are many more where these came from."

"Many, did you say?" She beamed at him. "But that is marvelous. You can distribute them to all the women whose husbands have been arrested or killed by the Nazis. It will be a godsend. That is," she added with her infallible courtesy, "if it is agreeable to you to do so."

"I will see to it," Paul promised. How discreet she was! She had not once asked where he had found this treasure trove of tin cans.

She had just placed his gift in her cupboard when there was a rap on the door. Paul opened it. Robert, accompanied by a gendarme, was standing outside. For a moment his heart sank. Nowadays the appearance of a gendarme at one's door was almost as frightening as the arrival of the Gestapo. But the gendarme greeted them with disarming friendliness.

"*Bonjour,* my boy . . . mademoiselle. Forgive my intrusion but I met Monsieur Robert on his way home and he seemed a little upset. These days, with the Germans everywhere, one doesn't know what to expect. I thought I'd better make sure he got home safely."

"How kind of you, monsieur," said Mademoiselle Ricard. "Do come in. Won't you have a cup of tea?"

"I won't say no." The gendarme sat down in an easy chair as Robert shuffled to his chaise longue. "My cousin married an Englishman and I visited them in England once. A strange country. They don't serve wine with their meals. But I learned to like tea."

"Will you excuse me, mademoiselle?" interrupted Paul. "I have some chores to do at home."

"But of course," she said. "Oh, I almost forgot. I've corrected your last week's English theme." She went again to the cupboard and brought out a paper. "Here it is. . . . I'm tutoring Paul afternoons, monsieur, since he's been working," she explained to the gendarme. "You did quite well, Paul, but you still get your verbs mixed. You must write, 'I am gone,' not 'I am go.' "

What a clever imagination she has, thought Paul.

"Let me take a look," asked the gendarme. "I'd like to see how much English I remember."

"Forgive me, monsieur. I'd be too ashamed." Paul held on to the paper tightly.

"Very well." The gendarme shrugged. "Next time maybe."

"Yes, next time," Paul promised as casually as he could.

"I will go to the corner with you," announced the schoolteacher. "It's getting dark and the street along here is full of holes. I'll be back in a minute, monsieur. Pour yourself another cup of tea."

As she walked along at Paul's side, she chattered: "The gendarme is so nice. So very nice. I can't think anything bad of him. It's so difficult to remember they're working for Vichy now—and so for the Germans. That was a very close shave. I'm afraid I was a bit indiscreet. You got out of it nicely, Paul. Good night now."

Paul hastened his steps until he reached the crossroads in front of the Monument des Morts, the monument put up for the veterans killed in the previous war. It was deserted now in the early dusk, and as he stood looking up at it he felt a pang of sorrow for those soldiers who had died so young, also that France might be free.

A small shadow came from around the side of the Monument. "Good evening, Paul."

"You're on time, Jeannot."

"We cannot be late for this sort of appointment," said his friend. "But then you know that."

"I know," Paul assured him, thinking what a chance he had taken to go exploring on that day, and what a lot of explaining he would have had to do had the door to the room under the Town Hall remained sealed. No more would he take such risks.

"Here's your letter, Jeannot." He handed him the paper given him by Mademoiselle Ricard.

"Good work, Paul."

The so-called "corrected English theme" was a coded message, and the gentle Mademoiselle Ricard was the established "post office" for the Moyelle Patriots. As one person whom the Nazis would never suspect of "terrorist" activities, she received important instructions from a larger Resistance organization, for which Paul was now serving his apprenticeship as official courier.

CHAPTER 6

A DAY IN THE MINES

"Don't worry, my boy. The work is hard but you'll get used to it." That was what Felix Virel, to whom Paul was assigned as helper, had told him his first day in the mines. Felix was right. Now, three months later, Paul was actually beginning to feel like an old-timer, able to take the daily routine in his stride.

At four o'clock in the morning, this cold day of early December, he was wakened by his mother's call. "Your coffee is ready, Paul." It was still dark at a quarter to five when he rode up to the mine gate on the bicycle that had been his father's and with his father's lunch bag hanging from a strap over his shoulder.

"*Bonjour*, Henri," he sleepily greeted the gate guard. "How goes it?"

"A little better, a little worse. I can't complain." Henri shrugged, and in so doing, coughed. He was a victim of silicosis, caused by stone dust lodged in the lungs, and though he would never get well and could never again do heavy labor, with proper care his life-span might extend for some years.

There were two German sentinels stationed at the mine entrance, but like the other miners pouring in at this hour, Paul ignored them. Parking his bicycle, he dashed full speed for the *lavabo,* the building where the men changed clothes and took their showers. There, in a long hall known by the gruesome name of "The Hanging Room," the miners' clothes hung from the ceiling on ropes attached to pulleys, each with a number and a lock. Paul, with the skill of practice, had the pulley unlocked and his wearing apparel down in no time—the blue denim trousers and jacket, sweater and neck scarf, the rope-soled espadrilles, the metal helmet which the French call a *barette.*

After he had changed, he stood in line to get his miner's lamp, which he attached by a clasp to his shoulders. The lamps were numbered too and the time they were picked up noted. If a lamp was not returned at the proper hour, the attendant would send out an alarm for a missing miner.

There was another dash then, across the yard to the pit entrance, where his fellow miners were congregated waiting for the elevator. Roland and Jeannot were there before him. Their greetings were shy and almost distant, as if to hide from the world the close bond between them. The older men on the contrary, even at this early hour, were laughing and kidding, giving the impression they had not a care in the world.

"Well now, Paul, how's the *galibot* this morning?" a miner called to him. "Galibot" was the name given to all young apprentice miners, and Paul assured the man that this *galibot* was on top of the world.

"I'm glad to hear it, my boy," the miner said heartily. "We have need of young people who keep on top of the world, no matter how hard others try to push them beneath it."

Was there a double meaning in his words? Was he too a Patriot—a member of the group with whom Jeannot alone had contact? Paul asked himself that question about everyone now, though he never tried to find out. He had learned well the lesson of secrecy.

A moment later they were all squeezing into the elevator, a rickety cage with open iron grilling. Down and down it plunged at a terrifying speed, swinging from side to side and occasionally banging against the walls of the shaft. Paul on his first trip had been so frightened that his companions had burst out laughing at the expression on his face. "The cable has never broken yet so why should it do so now?" they asked, not too reassuringly. Before the war the union had been petitioning for a new elevator but all such requests were ignored for the duration.

With a jolt it came to a halt about a quarter of a mile beneath the earth's surface. The door opened and they stepped forth into a strange underground city, a city of blackness without streetlamps or growing things, a city made up of a maze of passageways through which only an expert could find his way. Miners shouted greetings to other miners as they emerged. The underground was a man's world, filled with men's voices with men's lusty humor and spicy talk, very far indeed from the softening influence of mothers and wives.

"Ah, there you are, my boy." Felix, who was talking with some comrades, came over to Paul. "Suppose we start our trek." Felix was a tall gaunt man with large callused hands, dark hair sprinkled with gray, irregular features, and roughened skin streaked with those slender blue marks which are the insignia of a miner's trade. His voice was kindly, and his manner was gently humorous.

Paul followed him down the main gallery, cut in stone,

with Roland and Jeannot and the others behind them.
Soon they turned into a side gallery hardly wider than the
tracks of the coal trains, ducking overhead cables, strad-
dling flooded areas with one foot on each track, agilely
avoiding other perils. A quarter of a mile of this and then
suddenly Felix vanished for all the world as though the
earth had swallowed him. Actually, he had swung onto a
ladder alongside a shaft leading to a lower level. Paul
scrambled after him like a monkey.

They climbed down a dozen more ladders before they
reached the level on which they worked. Nor was their
journey over yet. In and out they went through a labyrinth
of tunnels, some so low they had to inch their way along
like earthworms. It grew increasingly hot and sweat
streamed from their faces. As soon as they began work they
would all strip to the waist.

"Here's Jacqueline, waiting for us impatiently," Felix
announced at last. "Jacqueline" was the name of the tunnel they were working.

"See you later," Paul called to Jeannot and Roland.
Jeannot was working in the next tunnel, which was called
"Thérèse." Roland was assigned to a still more distant
point. The Engineer had made sure that these three sons of
"troublemakers" should not work together.

Felix got out their tools and arranged them carefully.
Even when this was done, he seemed in no hurry to start.
"I think we'd better check the props," he said.

The props were the wooden poles, upright and hori-
zontal, which supported all the tunnels except the stone
galleries. They were the protection against the countless
tons of earth and rock pressing down from above. On their
solidity depended the safety and the lives of the working
miners. Before the war the men had resented the time

spent to test them, since they were paid only for the coal they mined. Since the Germans had taken over, however, they had become increasingly concerned with the state of the props, examining them minutely every day.

Felix and Paul were still working on the props when Gustave Groja came by on his daily tour. Gustave was the delegate; his job was to bring to the Engineer the miners' grievances and to make sure personally that all safety regulations were in force. Felix had been delegate before the war, elected to that post by the members of the miners' union. The Germans had ousted Felix and appointed Gustave in his place. Gustave came from Alsace and the men said of him that even if he did not have German blood he had the heart of a Nazi. Within the union, even before the war, he had been known as a stool pigeon.

"Good morning, Gustave," Felix said casually as he approached.

"What are you doing?" demanded the delegate, a lean sallow-faced man with a habitually sour expression.

"You can see for yourself. The props are in a dangerous condition. We're fixing them."

"You were doing that yesterday," Gustave grumbled.

"They were dangerous yesterday," Felix stated cheerily.

"You spend more time on the props than on digging coal."

"That's not your concern, my friend." Felix's voice was coolly sarcastic. "You are allegedly working for us. Remember? By the way, did you tell the Engineer there was too much loose coal dust around here?"

"I did," said Gustave sulkily.

"He must not have heard you because the coal dust is still here."

"Is it my fault?" demanded Gustave. "Am I supposed to sweep it up?"

"A little work now and then does no man any harm," commented Felix, his face expressionless.

Gustave flushed. "Be careful how you talk to me."

"You intend to report me? On what grounds? For looking out for the interests of the Company? Go ahead."

Gustave started to stamp off in a temper but Felix called him back.

"Just a second, Gustave. How is it you carry an electric lamp instead of an oil one? You know the union regulations."

"Union regulations!" snorted Gustave. "A lot they mean now."

"Gustave!" Felix's voice was sharp. "I know what you are and you know that I know. No matter. You still have a certain responsibility and there's going to be trouble if you don't watch out."

"Mind your own business," muttered Gustave, furious.

When he was gone, Paul asked curiously, "What did you mean about the oil lamp, Felix?"

"Every delegate is supposed to carry an oil lamp on his tour," explained Felix. "As he enters each tunnel he holds it high. If the fire flares up, that's a sign that gas is seeping in. Gas is perhaps the greatest danger in any mine. You can't see it but a spark will cause it to explode."

Felix had worked in the mines since he was ten and knew nearly everything there was to know about mining. Under present conditions, he had no scruples about taking time off to instruct Paul.

"You must become a good miner," he frequently said to him. "After the war, France is going to need a lot of coal."

Sometimes when they were alone, he talked about what

the mines had been like in the time of their grandfathers. The workday was twelve hours long in those days and many saw daylight only on Sundays. Women and children, even babes no more than five and six, worked beside the men in the pit. There were no pensions, sick pay, nor accident compensation. Because labor was cheap and plentiful, the Company was indifferent to the health and welfare of their miners. Even the mine horses received better care.

After the miners formed a union, conditions began to improve, Felix said. It happened gradually, and every pay increase, every decrease in working hours, every installation of safety measures, was the result of long negotiations and often of bitter strikes.

"Before the Germans came, miners were beginning to live as men should," Felix added. "We earned a living wage and worked a 48-hour week. Our wives did not have to work. Beginning in 1936, we were granted two-week vacations with pay. The miners went wild with delight. For the first time, they had a chance to visit some of the beautiful spots in France, the forests of the Vosges, the beach at Le Touquet, the Riviera, the Pyrenees, places once reserved solely for wealthy tourists.

"The Germans want to take all these benefits away from us. It's our job to see they don't succeed." He added, "It's also up to us to see they don't strip our mines of coal."

He had said no more at the time but on subsequent occasions he dropped hints as to how production might be slowed up without attracting attention. Nor did he always think in terms of minor sabotage.

"Paul, did you know that a huge cache of dynamite is kept on the seventh level?" he asked casually one day. "We use it for blasting. A funny thing. Every time I think of that dynamite I think of how many enemy tanks it would destroy."

In a sense, working with Felix was like going to school. Paul learned something new every day. Yet what a strange situation for him! He was on his first job and in one way wanted desperately to make good. The trouble was that if he worked too hard, he would be helping the enemy. His only consolation was that after the war, it would be different.

Paul's reflections were suddenly interrupted by a loud *"Miouw!"* He looked around and saw two great round orange orbs staring out at him from the black depths beyond his lamp.

"What's that?" he asked.

Felix grinned. "You have not met our mascot? Baboule lives here. We used to bring her milk every day but now she has to be satisfied with scraps. She has her job too. If it weren't for her, the rats would get your lunch before you did. . . . Here, pussy, come meet Paul."

The big cat, lean and gray, came out of the shadows and let Felix stroke her with his large blackened hands. "People say that miners are hard," he said as he caressed her. "But we all love Baboule. She too is part of our life in the mines."

Paul watched him with admiration. Felix was strong and unafraid, but beneath his rough exterior he was tender, too. He imagined himself telling his own father how much Felix had taught him, and he could almost hear his father saying, "So you're a real miner now, Paul. I'm proud of you."

"And now to work," Felix said. "There is no miner yet born able to live wholly on love and fresh air." Baboule retreated back into her lair, and Felix rose and picked up the cumbersome *marteau-piqueur,* the compressor drill, handling it like a child's toy. With the handle pressed against his chest, he turned it against the wall of coal, then switched on the power, causing lumps of coal to tumble down. It was Paul's job to stack them for the conveyor belt, which would in turn take them to the coal cars.

The drilling was not easy. Paul had tried it once. Not only had he barely been able to lift the drill; when the power was on he jumped as if an electric shock had hit him. The nearby miners had burst out laughing.

"Never mind," Felix consoled him. "You'll master it in time. After you've grown a bit bigger and stronger. In America, they use machines to get the coal, but their coal galleries are wide and high. Our large veins are mined out so the machines are useless. We have to do the best we can."

The compressor drills made a deafening roar. It was impossible to talk. Work continued until nine-thirty when the siren blew. This was the signal for the midmorning snack, a half-hour rest period known as the *briquet.* The miners put aside their drills, opened their lunch bags, taking out the sandwiches prepared by their wives and the thermos bottles filled with a mixture of unsweetened cold coffee and water, and squatted down on their heels to eat. Jeannot came over from Thérèse to join them. Now they could relax, however briefly, tell stories, joke with each other, or give vent to complaints that had been damming up inside of them.

One of them had been away on sick leave for a week.

"You weren't sick, Jojo," a comrade ribbed him. "You just wanted to stay home with your wife."

"On the contrary I was very ill," announced Jojo gravely. "I had a cold in the head."

"So? I remember the time when pneumonia would hardly keep you away. That was of course before the war."

Taking advantage of sick leave was one way of plaguing the Nazis. Whereas once they ignored small wounds and minor illnesses, now even a bruised finger gave a man an excuse to ask for a week's layoff.

Though the miners accepted the danger of their daily life with a shrug and a laugh, they grumbled bitterly over little things. Today as every day they raged against the gray and tasteless bread.

"It is fit for pigs." A miner rolled some crumbs into a sticky ball, threw it on the coal dust and stamped on it. "Not good enough for pigs. It's only suitable for Nazis."

"When are we going to see white loaves again?" This was a daily lament.

Once their thick sandwiches of white bread had been filled with butter, cheese, or *pâté*. Now they were lucky if they had pork fat to spread on the unappetizing slices. Today, the La Coques' weekly rations being near exhaustion, Paul had only sliced carrots between his bread. Jeannot, he noticed, had no bread at all, only two small boiled potatoes. How could anyone do a day's work on such a diet?

"Do me a favor, Jeannot. Eat one of my sandwiches. I can't swallow any more."

"I don't believe you, Paul."

Paul shrugged. "Take it. Or else I'll give it to Baboule. And Baboule has no liking for either bread or carrots."

Reluctantly as Jeannot accepted the morsel, he devoured it ravenously. There were still a few minutes of freedom left. They rose and walked off to stretch their legs.

"You want to know what I've decided, Paul?" the younger boy confided unexpectedly. "I've decided to be a writer."

"A writer?" To Paul, writers were fabulous beings from another world, very unlike the little black-faced gnome at his side. "What ever would you write about?"

"About us." Jeannot's voice was earnest. "I think people should know about the coal miners. How hard they work and how brave they are. How they are both strong and goodhearted. How they come to work when it's still night and go home so tired they're hardly aware whether the sun is shining or a storm raging. How the miners' wives scrub and cook so that everything at home is clean and warm and pretty. Does that sound silly to you?"

"No, it doesn't sound silly." Paul hesitated. "Only it never occurred to me that anyone would want to know about our lives."

"Maybe not, but I'd like to write it anyway. Sometimes when I'm working I think of the sky and the mountains and singing birds and things like that. I've never seen the ocean even though it's less than fifty miles away. I don't know quite how to explain it but just by thinking about these things, it seems to me my thoughts bring them to me."

"I guess I see what you mean." Paul had suddenly become aware of a new side to his friend, as one might pick up a stone which looked like all other stones but which, when one turned it over, was sparkling and shining gold. But with his realization of a new depth in Jeannot's character came a spasm of jealousy, not unlike that which he had felt on first learning that Jeannot knew more about the Resistance than he did. "You are the brainiest of us all, little Jeannot," he said again, to still that unpleasant feeling.

"I want to show you something I wrote." Jeannot took

from his pocket a sheet of cheap notepaper with some pencil scribbling. "You may laugh but I wanted you to see it."

The siren sounded, announcing that their half-hour break was over. Paul shoved the paper into his pocket. "I'll read it after work. Thanks, Jeannot."

According to the mine routine, the men would now work straight through until one-thirty, the end of the morning shift. Then they would head back to the elevator, ride up to the earth's surface, and file into the shower room. Today Paul would ride his bicycle home. Other times, when his mother needed it for some errand or other, he would walk. Either way, as soon as he entered the kitchen he could be sure that his mother would have soup on the table for him —just as she always had served it for his father.

Today this daily routine was to be varied, like a play whose director decides, after many identical rehearsals, that a new scene is needed. And in this play, about a day in the mines, fate had decreed that the new scene be a tragic one.

At five minutes past eleven on that Saturday morning in December, the harsh buzzing of the drills, the men's shouts and cries, the rumbling of the conveyor belt engine—all the ordinary sounds of the mine—were deadened by a crash like a thunderbolt. How could there be thunder in a mine? That was Paul's first irrational thought. Then some unseen force knocked him to the ground.

A moment later smoke filled the tunnels and all was confusion.

"Explosion in Thérèse!" someone shouted.

That was where Jeannot was working.

Still half-stunned, Paul pulled himself to his feet and headed down the narrow winding passageway to the tunnel Thérèse, sliding and half falling in his haste. Miners running from that direction yelled at him, but he slipped past, paying them no heed, until he reached the tunnel entrance, beyond which was an inferno of flames and smoke.

There is a very slim line between bravery and foolhardiness. Which motivated Paul he could not have said. He only knew that he had to reach Jeannot, no matter what, but as he was about to plunge into the flames someone grabbed him around the waist.

"You can't go in there, my boy."

He struggled futilely against Felix's strong arms. "Let me go. Jeannot . . ."

"No one can go in there and live." Felix's voice was firm. "The salvage crew will be here soon. We must wait for them."

"Soon it will be too late." Paul, still fighting to free himself, unconsciously quoted old Robert.

"There is no choice, Paul. You must save yourself, for your father and for France." He dragged the still-resisting lad back a safe distance from the fire. "Here's your jacket. Quick. Use it as a broom to clean up the coal dust here. We must make a barrier to keep the fire from spreading."

Paul obeyed automatically. Neither the foreman nor Gustave had made an appearance. It was Felix who had taken charge, directing the men where to go and what to do, stilling panic, giving commands reasonably and reassuringly.

At last the salvage crew arrived with their fire-fighting equipment and their oxygen masks. It was not long—though it seemed so to Paul—until they had the fire, which Felix's quick thinking had kept from spreading, under control. From the smoldering wreckage they brought out the first victim, then another and another, until there were five in all—the last one, little Jeannot.

Paul knelt beside the blackened form that had so recently held the spirit of his friend. He shook with sobs.

"Come." Felix stooped to pick up Jeannot's body gently in his arms. "We will take him back."

The long trip with their sad burden, through tunnels, up ladders and to the elevator, was for Paul a blur of horror. Afterwards he could never remember how they managed it. When they came out into the open air, it was snowing, the first snowstorm of the year. A stretcher was waiting and someone placed Jeannot on it and someone else covered him with a blanket. Felix and Paul carried it between them, the white snowflakes melting on their black faces and garments.

At the mine gate, the women of Moyelle were gathered anxiously. They had poured from their homes when the loud mine siren announced the catastrophe, clad in housedresses with thin sweaters over their shoulders, barelegged, wearing carpet slippers or wooden shoes.

As the gate opened to let Felix and Paul out, Madame Virel, Felix's wife, a sweet-faced woman with soft graying hair, rushed up to him, throwing her arms around his neck. Madame La Coque did not seem to recognize Paul and hesitated, staring at him doubtfully.

"Mother, it is I. Paul."

"Oh, thank heavens." She breathed deeply in relief.

Two other mothers had hold of him.

"And Roland?"

"And Jeannot?"

"Jeannot is here, madame." Paul indicated the stretcher. He knew no way to soften the blow for Madame Du Bois and though he searched for words to comfort her, he could not find them. With a shriek she sank to the ground beside her oldest son.

"And Roland? Paul, where is Roland?" Madame Michel's hazel eyes were wide and frightened.

"I think he is safe," Paul said to reassure himself as much as to calm his friend's mother.

Wordlessly they waited, the falling snow cloaking their sorrow in a white mantle. More miners emerged, some carrying other victims, and more women cried with joy or with grief. At the very last, Roland appeared, a sturdy black figure, walking unsteadily. Madame Michel did not recognize him either.

"There's Roland," Paul said.

Then she was touching Roland's face, holding him to her until she too was smudged with coal, almost as black as he.

"We were trapped above the explosion," Roland summed up his experience briefly. "It took the salvage crew a time to get us out."

Someone had already told him about Jeannot. For a moment he stood before the stretcher, tears streaking his face. Then they all started walking, with Madame Du Bois, Paul, Roland and Felix carrying the stretcher.

At home, after the heartrending scene, Paul washed in a washtub, which his mother filled with hot water, as miners had done in the days before the luxury of shower rooms. In disgust, he kicked his miner's clothes in a corner. He never wanted to see them again. In a clean shirt and trousers he sat down at the table. His mother tried vainly to get him to eat his soup.

"I'm not hungry, Mother." Paul pushed the plate away.

"You need it, my darling." She rarely used tender words to her son; it was not the custom. "You will eat now and I will tell you the good news—for there is seldom so dark a day that it does not give a ray of hope, and this has happened today. We have a card from your father."

"From Father? Where is he?"

She handed the card to him. "He is at a prison in Vught, Holland. At least he is not in Germany and that is something to be thankful for. I am well, he wrote. I think often of you. Kiss Mitzi and Emile for me and embrace Paul. I know he is looking after you." She had memorized it all. "It is not much but it is better than silence."

"And Roland's father?" questioned Paul, after a moment.

"They are still together. Hélène received a card today too. They cannot write much or often, but it is good to know where they are."

"It is good," agreed Paul, though even this news could not drown his pain at the fate of his small comrade. He rose and picked up his coal-black jacket, searching in the pockets until he found the sheet of notepaper Jeannot had given him that morning.

"What's that, Paul?"

"It's something Jeannot wrote." He studied the scrawling handwriting. "It's called 'Flowers.' "

"Flowers?" His mother's expression was wistful. "It is a long time since I have thought of flowers. Why don't you read it aloud, Paul?" While she listened, she picked up her sewing, some garment she was altering for a merchant's wife—her way of contributing to the family income since Paul would not let her work in the beet fields.

"Flowers, like the birds, come to mark the change of the seasons," Paul read slowly. "The first ones, in delicate hues, come with the swallows. The last, in brilliant reds and blues and orange, come with the crows to announce the end of the fine days and the beginning of winter. During the cold weather, they rest, hidden and waiting, ready to burst forth again when the warmth of spring creeps into the air. Flowers have many uses in our lives. They are given to celebrate a birthday or a wedding. Alas, they serve also to cover the tombs of the dead."*

He looked up to see tears streaming down his mother's face.

"Do not cry," he said softly. "Jeannot liked to think of the beautiful things we could not see in the mine. His thoughts made them real—as real as the coal."

The funeral for the victims of the catastrophe was held three days later in a joint public ceremony, following the individual church services. The coffins, banked with wreaths, were placed in front of the Town Hall. In the square, nearly all the citizens of Moyelle were gathered, along with delegations from neighboring mining towns— Liévin, Avion, Lens, Hénin-Liétard, Courrières—come to show their sympathy. A drizzling rain was falling as if the heavens were weeping with the bereaved. A few of the assembly carried umbrellas but most seemed unaware of the drops that fell on their coats and the hats which they wore only for church or such occasions as this.

Around each coffin were the watchers, chosen from the closest comrades of the miners who had died. By Jeannot's coffin were Paul and Roland, wearing clean miners' denims and their metal helmets, and Carlo and Gaston, in ordinary suits. All four stood solemnly, their heads high, like soldiers on duty.

*This piece on flowers was actually written by a young French miner, Henri Des Fresnes, who at the age of sixteen perished in a mine accident similar to the one described in this chapter.

The first shock of Jeannot's death had given way in Paul's mind to the bitter realization that he would never see or talk with him again, never ride down the elevator with him in the early morning, nor meet him in the Chamber of the Underground. How he would miss him! How unfair it was that he should have been taken from them!

The ceremony opened with a speech by the Mayor. He was not the mayor elected by the people before the war, who was now in prison. This new mayor, a tall bony man, bald-headed, with a black goatee, had been sent by the Vichy Government, the former French leaders who now gave allegiance to the Nazis. Paul had only contempt for him and hardly listened as he rattled off a stereotyped speech beginning, "We come together on this sad occasion . . ."

Next came Monsieur Beaulieu, the Engineer, who spoke in much the same manner, except that he began, "It is with the deepest regret . . ." Nevertheless, Paul sensed a difference between the attitude of the Engineer and that of the Mayor. He seemed genuinely upset, and though he was certainly an experienced speaker, several times he stammered and hesitated, as if tempted to say something quite different from his prepared talk. Paul remembered the Engineer's telephone conversation with the Kommandant the day he had applied for a job. Though Beaulieu had warned the Kommandant about the undue amount of coal dust in the galleries, he had not been too insistent when the Kommandant had minimized the danger. Did the Engineer perhaps feel guilty?

The next speaker was Felix. Paul and the other miners had signed a petition, asking that he be allowed to speak instead of Gustave, who as delegate would normally have been chosen for the honor, but they had not expected their request to be granted. Why had it been? Paul suspected that the Engineer, realizing the hatred against Gustave, had thought it unwise at this moment to add to the men's resentment.

Felix spoke simply in the patois of the miners. He talked of each of the victims in turn, coming finally to Jeannot. "Jeannot was not yet thirteen, the youngest of all," he said. "Though he was small and not strong, he laughed at the hardships of the miner's life and reported to duty each day with the gaiety and courage of his youth. We loved Jeannot. His loss is not only for his family but for all of us."

Paul expected that Felix would be the last of the speakers but there was one more of whom none of them had been told. To his astonishment he saw Kommandant Schmidt go up to the speaker's stand, a German adjutant on each side of him. Apparently the Kommandant had decided that this would be a good chance to show that he too was an important personage in the town affairs.

He began his speech correctly enough: "My heart bleeds with the good people of Moyelle today for the loss they haf so griefously suffered." The word "heart" was one in fact that he used repeatedly. "Your happiness is nearest to my heart," he had the audacity to assert. And later, "With all my heart I pray for the families of those who have been severed from mortal life."

Paul sensed an unrest among the mourners. People began to move around and talk in low voices to each other. But the Kommandant, unconcerned by the lack of interest, continued to spout his hypocritical phrases. Finally he got to the point. "We Germans," he stated, "devote ourselves *heart* and soul to the welfare of the French miners, as dear to us as our own brothers. Alas, our efforts are useless without cooperation. The rules of the Company are made for

the good of all. When irresponsible persons disobey regulations, it is they who must suffer. . . ." His voice rose to a
shriek.

Paul stiffened with fury. The Kommandant, knowing
very well that the accident was the result of the neglect of
the Company and the German directors, was accusing the
miners themselves! The vague unrest among the mourners
changed to an outraged murmur. The gendarmes, stationed
at intervals around the square, put their hands to their
holsters, as if expecting a riot. Someone shouted out, "It is
a lie," and others took up the cry. Trouble seemed inevitable.

Then Felix stood up in his place on the speakers' stand
and raised his hand in a commanding gesture. "My
friends," he said clearly and loudly, "remember why we are
here today. Remember the respect due to those who have
been taken from us." That was all, but his words caused the
people to quiet down immediately. The danger was
averted. The hearses drove up, the coffins were loaded in,
and the long slow march to the cemetery began.

CHAPTER 7

THE AFFAIR OF THE
BREAD COUPONS

The activities of the Club of Young Patriots, in the first months of its existence, were varied, if not spectacular. On a toy printing press which Gaston had donated, they printed VIVE DORETTE on scraps of paper, right after a woman named Dorette had tried to assassinate the collaborationist Pétain. The printed slips materialized all over town. The boys sold paper butterflies with the letter *V* (for Victory) inscribed on them for five francs each, turning the money over to Jeannot to pass on to his contact. They rummaged for paper, as scarce as other commodities in occupied France, collecting wrapping paper, old menus, even funeral and wedding announcements provided they were blank on one side, cutting them in neat stacks so they could be used for leaflets informing the people about matters they could not learn from the Vichy press.

On occasion they were called on to distribute the finished leaflets.

Singly or together they went out to the country on their

bicycles, ostensibly to try to buy eggs, milk or butter from the farmers, but also to make deliveries to persons in neighboring villages whose names and addresses they had memorized.

On the whole, the Club members worked well together. Paul was the accepted leader, though tactfully he never made a decision without consulting all of them. Roland was second in command. He had a talent for solving practical problems and planning the best and easiest way to get things done. Carlo, who had an inventive mind, was full of ideas. His fiery temperament was combined with a fervent hatred of the Nazi conquerors, and no day was complete to him unless he was able to do something to make them uncomfortable. Gaston had a calm nature and was able to see the amusing side of every situation. No matter how tired they were, he was always able to do or say something to rouse their spirits. But Jeannot had been the soul of their group.

His death had a sobering effect on the others. They had become increasingly anxious to have something really important to do. But who would be their contact now that Jeannot was gone?

Paul was wondering about this one afternoon as he was waiting in line at the Cooperative for bread. This was one household chore he did himself whenever he could. One still had to stand in line at least an hour and usually longer. It was too fatiguing for his mother, who had not been strong since Mitzi's birth. Also he could listen to the conversation around him, and from what people said judge which of them he dared approach to buy his V butterflies.

"Hello, Paul."

He turned and saw Lucette, Jeannot's older sister, standing behind him.

Guiltily, because he had not been to see the Du Bois family since Jeannot's funeral, he began to apologize.

Lucette interrupted him. "I know how it is. You have no time. That's one effect of the Occupation. Everyone is so busy they have no time to pay visits."

"Are you still working at Roubaix, Lucette?"

"Yes, there's no factory work here in Moyelle. Mother's working in the beet fields." She looked uncomfortable. "I told her she ought not, but she insisted. I catch my bus for Roubaix at three in the morning and Mark takes charge until I get home at three in the afternoon. Gilbert and Gilberte help with the cleaning and cooking. They do their best, but you can imagine what goes on."

"I'll drop in and have a look one of these days," Paul promised.

"The neighbors are scandalized that we leave the little ones alone," Lucette continued. "But what else can we do? Nobody has offered to look after them for us."

Jeannot's older sister was a nice-looking girl with sandy bobbed hair, large blue eyes, and white skin. People said of her that she was conscientious and hard-working but that she was temperamental. Her talkativeness today was surprising. Usually she treated Paul with the disdain of any girl of her age for a boy a year younger than herself.

At last Paul was at the head of the line. As the clerk cut off a chunk of bread and weighed it on the scales to make sure he had no more and no less than the amount to which his bread coupons entitled him, Lucette whispered, "Wait for me, Paul. I'll walk up the street with you."

"If you wish, Lucette." Paul was puzzled and, to tell the truth, annoyed. Should any of his comrades at the mine see him walking with a girl, he would be sure to get a ribbing.

"Wait outside," Lucette repeated. She spoke softly but her voice was urgent.

She joined him as soon as she had her bread, and as they strolled up the street she continued to talk, rather too loudly, about the problems of looking after a household of small children and holding a job as well. Then, abruptly, she lowered her voice.

"I won't beat around the bush, Paul. I asked you to meet me because I want to join your Club of Young Patriots."

"What do you mean?" he stalled, shocked and worried.

"You know what I mean. Jeannot told me all about it."

Paul was at a loss for words. "But Lucette . . . the club is for men. Women . . . well, they just don't belong."

"Women don't belong!" she repeated after him scornfully. "There are a lot of things you don't know, Paul La Coque. What would you think if I told you that all over France, girls and women are working in the Resistance against the Nazis—yes, right along with the men. Even here in Moyelle . . ." She stopped as though she had said too much. "Anyway, in Moyelle men always have been old-fashioned in their ideas about women. You, like the rest. You think women are good only to keep house."

"It's not that," protested Paul, though in fact Lucette had hit the nail on the head. He did feel women belonged in the home.

"You needn't look so upset." Lucette shifted her bread to the other arm. "I shan't attend your meetings, except if there's an emergency. You see . . . I've been instructed to act as your contact."

This was startling news. "You? Our contact?" He did not want to believe it, but he knew one thing about Lucette. She always told the truth. "Well, that's fine, Lucette," he said lamely.

"We have a job for your Club," Lucette went on. "Listen carefully, Paul. The town has just received a supply of bread coupons. They're in a safe in the Town Hall basement. There's only one guard—a pensioned gendarme called Nicolas who sleeps there nights. Do you know him?"

"I think so," said Paul. "He spends most of his time drinking at cafés, doesn't he?"

"That's the one. They say he's a sound sleeper. You'll surely have to wake him to get him to unlock the safe. You must go in by your secret entrance from the tunnel. To-morrow night. The rest should be easy."

"If you say so, Lucette. But . . ."

"But what?"

"Is it right?" he blurted out. "I mean how about the people? If they don't have coupons, they can't get their bread."

"There's no problem there," she assured him. "When the Mayor reports the loss, new coupons will be sent. But Paul, even if it did mean hardship here, we'd have to go ahead with it. Some of those coupons will go to the families of the Patriots who have been shot or deported, not only in Moyelle but elsewhere. There are other uses for them—for men in hiding from the Nazis, for families who are shelter-ing Jewish children. You can be sure that for many, the coupons will mean the difference between life and death."

In her terse matter-of-fact way she gave him a few more instructions. "The rest is up to you. Here's where I leave you. Good-bye, Paul. Give my best to your mother." She held out her hand to him. As he took it, he felt something fall into his own hand.

At midnight the following day the four boys met at the Chamber of the Underground. They had all slipped out of their homes after their families had gone to bed, trusting as always that their mothers would not hear them, or that if they did, nothing would be said.

In spite of Roland's hopes, the old German Lugers had proved to be rusted beyond repair. Nevertheless, they had cleaned and polished them so they at least looked like dangerous weapons. On this night they could still be useful, and each boy took one for his own. Then Paul distributed black masks, souvenirs of the festival of Mardi Gras, as well as the German helmets, which would conceal their hair. Their disguises were complete.

Roland produced a rope. "I sneaked it out of the mines today."

"Good for you," Paul praised him. Roland, as usual, thought of everything.

Nervous as they were, they could not repress the feeling that the night's escapade would be a lark. Even when Paul made a little speech about the importance of their task and the need for caution and prudence, their spirits remained uncurbed.

"Good-bye, Fritz. Wish us luck," Gaston called out as they started down the tunnel. They had buried the German soldier of the First World War just outside the entrance to the Chamber, in that brief stretch where the walls were of packed dirt before they reached the sandstone walls of what Paul now called the Roman Road. They still addressed him as though he were a silent witness to their activities.

Without incident they reached the small room under the Town Hall, where they stopped to check their helmets and masks. Paul raised the trapdoor and listened. The safe was in a basement room over by the stairway but even at this distance they could hear old Nicolas snoring. All well so far. Lithely, Paul pulled himself up through the trapdoor, giving a hand to the others.

Roland tried the door to the storage room. "Locked!" he exclaimed in consternation.

"Our contact thought that it might be and prepared us for this emergency." Paul displayed the passkey which Lucette had given him when she shook hands with him. How had she managed to get it? There were many Patriots in Moyelle now; there might well be some within the Town Hall offices.

The door opened with a noisy creak but the snores of old Nicolas did not lessen. One by one they tiptoed along the hall until they came to where he was sleeping on an old army cot. They gathered around him in a circle, while Paul turned the flashlight on his face. Dressed in nightshirt and cap, the guard was sprawled on his back, his mouth wide open. The snores continued unevenly, now loud enough "to wake the dead," now subsiding into raucous whistling.

"What a beautiful picture!" said Paul, not bothering to lower his voice.

"A pity we don't have a camera," commented Gaston. "We could have his photograph framed and send it to his wife."

"All that and a free concert too," mocked Carlo.

"No laughing now," warned Paul. "Remember, this is war. Lieutenant, wake the prisoner."

Carlo, the "Lieutenant," extracted a straw from old Robert's broom, which was leaning against the wall, and tickled the sleeping man's nose. Nicolas grimaced, sneezed, and, still sleeping, reached up his hand as if to brush away a fly. Carlo repeated the tickling. Nicolas sneezed again, this time opening his eyes. He blinked, incredulous. Was

he dreaming? Were all those armed and masked bandits standing over him?

"What is this? Who are you? What do you want?" His voice was a terrified rasp.

"Quiet!" ordered Paul, doing his best to sound tough and stern. "Not a word if you want to save your skin."

"Ugh . . . ugh," sputtered Nicolas.

"Do as we tell you and you won't be hurt. Otherwise . . ." He brandished the Luger.

"Don't shoot!" pleaded the old man. "I'll do anything . . . anything you say."

"Get up and unlock the safe."

"Let me get dressed," moaned Nicolas, too petrified to move.

"As you are," snapped Paul. "Get going."

Trembling, Nicolas struggled out of bed.

"The keys now!"

"Yes, yes. To be sure." From beneath his pillow he pulled forth his key ring.

"All right now. On your feet!"

He was such a comical sight with his dangling white nightshirt and his hairy legs that it was hard for Paul to obey his own command not to laugh and he bit his lip to repress his giggles. "Hurry now. We don't have all night."

"Yes, messieurs. I never said I wouldn't." Fear forced his shaking hands to unlock the primitive safe.

"Now give me the bread coupons."

"Bread coupons?" Nicolas repeated in astonishment. "You only want the bread coupons?"

"You heard me."

"Yes, monsieur. Here they are. See for yourself."

Paul seized the package from his hand. "Take a look,

Captain," he addressed Gaston. "Make sure the prisoner is speaking the truth."

Gaston ripped open one side of the package as Paul turned the flashlight on it. Here they were, hundreds and hundreds of bread coupons, enough for a whole town for a month—and enough for an army of Patriots! Never had bandits been rewarded with such spoils.

"They are in order, General." Gaston spoke in a high falsetto.

"Excellent. Back to bed, old man," said Paul.

"You'll go now?" asked Nicolas hopefully.

"After we've made sure you can't follow us."

"You're not going to kill me!" Nicolas' legs gave way and he sank to his knees.

"You're not worth the killing." There was real contempt in Paul's voice now. "Get marching. Lie on the cot face down. Hands behind your back. Captain, you tie him up."

"Yes, General." Roland pulled out his rope from inside his jacket and with Gaston and Carlo tied the guard's hands and feet securely.

"This is for your own good, old man," Paul told him. "In order that you won't be accused of having done this job yourself. No sound, mind you, or things will go badly for you."

"Not a word," Nicolas promised tearfully into his pillow. "I don't want to die. I've done everything you said, haven't I? I won't tell anybody . . ." He was still mumbling his pleas as the boys quietly withdrew. Though they knew he was in no condition to pay attention, they retreated stealthily so that their footsteps would not indicate the direction they took. As they entered the storage room, a sixth sense warned Paul that someone was there.

"Stop," he whispered to his comrades, turning the flashlight from corner to corner. There, sitting on an old chair directly over the trapdoor, was Robert Ricard. He looked up at them placidly.

"Good evening," he said. "Soon it will be too late."

"What are you doing here, monsieur?" gasped Paul.

"I knew you would come," Robert rambled on, smiling gently. "I am glad. I can talk to you frankly because you are not of this world. People here think I am mad. Do you want to know why?"

The boys stared at each other, not knowing what to do or say.

"Once I shook hands with Death," Robert confided in a conspiratorial whisper. " 'Come, Robert. Soon it will be too late,' Death said to me. But then the men came with their picks and their lanterns and I had to go back to the living."

What was he trying to say? Paul decided he would have to figure that out another time. The important thing now was to get him out of the storage room.

"Robert," he said coaxingly. "Josephine wants you to sweep the floors for her. She is calling you. Go to her."

"Yes, yes." He rose docilely and shuffled out down the hall.

Paul locked the door after him and without further words the boys climbed down through the trapdoor. The encounter with the fear-crazed guard had been amusing, indeed quite a lark, but Robert's words had cast a spell over them and never had the tunnel seemed so filled with specters of the past. It was not until they were on the road back to town that their high spirits returned.

Gaston, assuming old Nicolas' abject attitude, went down on his knees in the middle of the road. "Don't shoot, my General, I beseech you. I will be good. I promise. I promise . . ."

"A vile traitor like you isn't worth shooting," Carlo proclaimed in his high falsetto. "Go and get drunk. It's all you're good for."

Paul too shared in the horseplay, in spite of a growing uneasiness which he did not wish to impart to the others. At the edge of town he left them. Before he could go home he had two errands to perform. The first was to leave the bread tickets in the hiding place which Lucette had designated. The second took him to Mademoiselle Ricard's "barrack." Going around to the back he knocked lightly on the window of her bedroom.

"Mademoiselle!" he called softly.

Unlike old Nicolas, she was not difficult to wake. Almost immediately she raised her window.

"Who is it?" he heard her gentle voice.

"It is I. Paul."

"Yes, yes, my boy. Come to the kitchen door and I'll let you in." She showed no surprise. Indeed it almost seemed to Paul that she had been expecting him.

"You look cold and tired." In her gray dressing robe and her soft graying hair over her shoulders, there was a misty quality about her, like a water spirit just arisen from the sea. "I'll have a cup of tea ready in a moment. It will do you good. I don't have to make a fire. I can use my Sterno. Friends in England sent it to me, have you ever seen it? The fire comes in a little can. You just lift the cover and set a match to it. Isn't it clever? The water boils rapidly."

Only when Paul had taken a swallow of the scalding brew, did she allow him to speak. "Now tell me, Paul, what's the matter?"

"It's about your brother, mademoiselle. You know that he was at the Town Hall tonight?"

She nodded. "Yes, he sometimes sleeps there. You know how Robert is. Stubborn as a child when he makes up his mind to something. Has anything happened to him?"

"Nothing yet." As briefly as possible, Paul told about the night's escapade and Robert's unwitting role in it.

She looked grave. "You're right to be concerned. They'll be sure to question him. It's true he has a few lucid periods. When he's alone with me he's sometimes almost rational. I never mention it because people have enough to gossip about as it is. What would happen if they put pressure on him, I cannot imagine. You say he did not see how you left?"

"No, we were careful to lock the door after him," Paul told her.

"I don't think he could tell them anything then. Unless he had known all along. It's hard to tell about Robert." She sighed and several tears formed in the corner of her eyes and rolled down over her cheeks, adding somehow to her mistly appearance. "If you had more experience in this work, you perhaps would not have taken a chance. You would have let my poor brother go to the Death he finds so tempting."

Paul stared at her, shocked. "You don't mean we should have . . ." He was unable to finish the sentence.

"Sometimes it's the kindest way." Her face was sad. "Many Patriots carry little pills with them just in case. Just in case the Gestapo gets hold of them and they fear they won't be able to stand what is done to make them betray their friends. There are times when death can be welcome. . . . But there's no use thinking of that now. We'll hope for the best and all our worries may be for nothing. Thank you for coming, Paul. Go home and try to get some sleep. Good night now."

A few days later Paul saw Lucette at the Cooperative. She looked at him with dancing eyes, bubbling over with some secret joke.

Again they walked home together. Paul no longer minded her company, though he had received a good bit of teasing at the mines about her. "Pretty young to go courting, aren't you, Paul? But then they always say that the young ones are the boldest." And much more in the same vein. Still it was much better to have the men think that Lucette was his girl friend than to guess at their real relationship.

"I could hardly wait to tell you," Lucette was saying. "One of our group stopped by the Café Maxim yesterday and there was old Nicolas in fine fettle. The proprietor was giving him drinks on the house. He was telling everybody how, single-handed, he defied eight giant-sized bandits, all wearing *horns!*"

Paul chuckled. "Come to think of it, he must have seen double. Eight instead of four of us, each twice life size. By horns he meant the spikes on the German helmets. He doubled up on them too!"

"I know what will happen," Lucette prophesied gleefully. "For years to come Nicolas will be telling his adventure to anyone who will buy him a drink. You will see. Eventually, it will be an army of a hundred or more whom he fought off so valiantly!"

It was good to see Lucette laughing, it happened so rarely. No wonder. With the life she led, she had little chance to enjoy herself. Today, with her eyes so sparkling, she looked really pretty.

For the moment Paul forgot what had been bothering him—that Robert was being held in the *gendarmerie* and that no one had been allowed to see him.

CHAPTER 8

THE TRAITOR

"I tell you I heard them, monsieur. With my own eyes."

Gustave, the delegate, was standing before the Engineer's desk, twisting his beret in his hands.

"If you can hear with your eyes, you're better than most of us," the Engineer said with a touch of sarcasm.

"You know what I mean, monsieur. I saw them and I heard them both—those two *galibots,* Paul La Coque and Roland Michel. They were making sandals for themselves out of pieces from the conveyor belt—and joking about it. This was just after the belt had broken down for the fourth time in the last month, and no way of transporting coal until it is fixed. If you ask my opinion, it didn't break at all. It was cut, by those two!" He started to spit, then, remembering where he was, restrained himself.

"I'm not interested in your opinions, Gustave, only in facts."

"Yes, monsieur, naturally," Gustave amended hastily. "As I said, they were joking. Roland said, 'I need these sandals badly.' 'What for?' Paul asked. And Roland told him, 'I need them to march in the victory parade the day France is free again.' "

"What did you do then?" asked Monsieur Beaulieu curiously.

"Why, I left quickly to come here, monsieur. I couldn't let them know I'd overheard, could I? One must be discreet, mustn't one?"

"Hmmm. I don't suppose you were afraid that if you were caught eavesdropping there might be a small accident? For instance, that a loose stone might have come tumbling down on your head as you were leaving?"

"Monsieur has a sense of humor," muttered Gustave uncomfortably.

"Was anyone else near them?"

The delegate's face brightened. "But yes, the miner, Felix Virel. He was not working too hard, in my opinion, not to know what they were doing. Does it not follow, monsieur, that if these *galibots* were engaged in sabotage of the conveyor belt, they might have something to do with the missing tools, perhaps even with the stoppage of the coal car engine a few weeks ago?"

"You have a point," admitted the Engineer, "but legally it doesn't follow. One crime is not *per se* evidence of another crime. Well, you've done your duty, Gustave. Get out now. I'm tired of looking at you."

"Yes, monsieur." Gustave backed out so hastily he stumbled and almost fell.

What an unsavory character, thought Monsieur Beaulieu as he watched him through his office window loping back toward the pit. The very air seemed polluted after he left. Unfortunately, he couldn't get rid of him. Informers—or as the German, Schmidt, called them, "men loyal to the Company"—did not grow on bushes these days. He shrugged and picked up the telephone.

"Operator. Get through to the foreman on the twelfth

level and tell him to send up the *galibots* Paul La Coque
and Roland Michel. At once."

Presently the boys came in, like two black sprites, standing very straight and looking at him questioningly.

"Well, boys, where are your sandals?" the Engineer demanded.

"Sandals, monsieur?" they asked, innocent as cherubs.

"Yes, sandals. The ones you made out of the conveyor
belt you chopped in two."

"I don't understand, monsieur," said Paul.

"Come now. You can't fool me. What did you do with
them? Hide them before you came up?"

"Hide what, monsieur?" Roland asked politely.

"Don't try to lie out of it. You were seen."

"I never lie, monsieur." Paul's voice was steady. "Unless
it is for my country."

The Engineer tried a different tactic. "You think I don't
know what you've been up to? Sabotage, you call it, and
feel pretty proud of yourselves. As though you'd done
something big. Pinpricks! A fly might as well try to kill a
giant by buzzing in its ear!"

"You are right, monsieur," Paul agreed. "Still, if there
were a thousand flies—or a hundred thousand—they could
do more than annoy that giant, couldn't they?"

The boy was not afraid to speak up to him. That was
sure.

Aloud, the Engineer said sternly, "There's such a thing
as being too clever, you know. I warn you. I don't want to
get any more bad reports about you. If I do, you'll be in
real trouble."

The boys knew what he meant. Men were shot these days
for less than they had done.

"Now get out both of you." The Engineer scowled. "Go on home. You'll be docked for the rest of the day."

Outside, the two boys gazed at each other in amazement. "I don't understand," said Roland. "Why did he let us off with just a scolding and an hour's docking?"

Paul shook his head. "It's too much for me. I thought our goose was cooked. That was Gustave's work. I'm sure of it."

After they had gone, the Engineer sat for a while looking unseeingly at the papers on his desk. Good boys those, like their fathers. If they had been his sons, he could have made something better than coal miners of them. But Colette, his wife, had never wanted children. With a sigh, he picked up the telephone.

"Get me Kommandant Schmidt."

"Yes, monsieur," came the operator's voice.

He hung up with a bang. That Kommandant with his bad manners, his abysmal ignorance of French culture and history, or of any culture and history, for that matter, except that of the Nazis. It was more than anyone could take. Anyone with self-respect, that is. Self-respect! The word pleased him, and he said it to himself several times. Suddenly he smiled—a slow determined sort of smile—and picked up the phone again.

"What are you doing?" he asked the telephone operator.

"I'm trying to put through your call to Kommandant Schmidt, monsieur."

"Schmidt! Who wants to talk to that lout? Cancel the call."

"Yes, monsieur." Her voice was impassive.

"Get Antoine, the foreman. No, I don't need to talk to him. Tell him to send up the miner Felix Virel. Got that?"

"Right away, monsieur."

When Felix ambled in a little later, the Engineer motioned him to a chair.

"I'd rather stand, monsieur. What's this about?"

"You've always been one of our best workers, Felix," the Engineer began in words that sounded pompous even to his own ears.

Felix eyed him quizzically. "You didn't have me come here to tell me that, monsieur."

"No, I didn't. I might as well give it to you straight, Felix. I have a paper here for your arrest."

"Oh, so that's it."

"There will be two gendarmes waiting for you at the gate when the first shift leaves."

"That's interesting. May I ask what the charges are?"

"If you wish." The Engineer read, from the paper on his desk: "Participation in illegal activities, organizing and heading a contingent of terrorists to conduct acts of rebellion against the government . . ."

"The Nazis word things impressively, don't they?" commented Felix. "I shall deny everything."

"It won't matter," Monsieur Beaulieu said. "They are certain to have witnesses."

Felix shrugged. "One takes life as it comes, monsieur. Thanks for telling me. *Au revoir.*" He turned to leave.

The Engineer held up his hand. "Felix, wait. Go sign off for the day. Say you're sick. These are my instructions. But don't turn in your lamp. Then go to the shower room. Get in the shower. Stay there or stay anywhere out of sight until after the second shift arrives. Don't leave until three o'clock or so. By then they'll have found out you reported sick and won't wait around any longer. Don't return to your home. It will be watched. Don't stay in Moyelle. It won't be safe."

Felix's calm was broken and he stared at Beaulieu in amazement. "Why, you've remembered you're a Frenchman!"

"Call it what you like," said the Engineer with an air of irritation. "If you want the truth I'm simply fed up with boorishness. Get going now, Felix. Good luck. Take this with you." He thrust out a thousand-franc note.

Felix didn't touch it. "I have no liking for charity, monsieur."

"Don't be a fool. This isn't charity. It's partial payment on a rather large debt I owe."

"Thanks then," Felix said, pocketing the note. "And good luck to you, too. You'll perhaps need it more than I."

When Paul reached home after being dismissed by the Engineer, a strange man was sitting in the kitchen, elderly, with short-cropped gray-streaked hair, a hawk nose, and skin as brown and wrinkled as the bark of a tree. Emile and Mitzi, usually such little devils, were standing watching him, a look of awed respect on their faces.

Even before presenting the stranger, his mother jumped up and cried, "What are you doing home so early? Has something happened?"

It's a funny thing about women, thought Paul. They make a scene if you come home late. They do the same if you arrive early. There's no suiting them.

"Nothing's happened, Mother. The Engineer gave us a little time off, that's all."

"But why? What had you done?"

"He said we'd been working too hard, we needed some rest. . . ."

"There, you see what a boy I have?" His mother turned

to the visitor. "Paul, say *bonjour* to your great-uncle. This is Uncle Georges from Sainte-Valérie."

So this was the famous great-uncle, so niggardly he sifted the ashes every morning to salvage a few morsels of coal!

"*Bonjour,* my uncle." He dutifully allowed himself to receive a dry peck on each cheek.

"Humph!" commented his uncle dourly. "Pale and skinny, isn't he?"

"All miners are pale," his mother said hastily, sensing Paul's resentment. "But he's strong, just like his father. You should feel his muscles, my uncle."

"Humph!" grunted the visitor again.

On the kitchen table, beside an old market basket of the sort peasants carried, were a bunch of leeks, four eggs, and half a pound of butter.

"Uncle Georges brought us these," said Madame La Coque brightly. "Wasn't it kind of him?"

The gifts were welcome but did not strike Paul as lavish. He, like other hungry townspeople, now looked on farmers as millionaires, with their cows and wheat fields and apple orchards.

"Thank you, my uncle," he said politely.

"He has just learned of Jules' . . . absence," continued Paul's mother. "He has come to offer to keep Emile and Mitzi on the farm. They will have milk and butter every day. Isn't he generous?"

"It's my duty to my kinfolk," said Uncle Georges shortly. "I never shirk my duty. The children wouldn't live another year here. Look at them! Skin and bones!"

Little Mitzi began to howl. "Mama, I'm not skin and bones. I'm a little girl, aren't I?"

Her mother took her up in her arms. "Of course you are, my little chicken. Uncle didn't mean anything."

"They're crybabies, too," commented Uncle Georges dourly. "I see I arrived just in time. A woman alone always spoils children. They'll get over that. Emile can learn to milk. Mitzi can help her aunt."

Paul was getting increasingly doubtful about the whole project. "Are you going to let them go, Mother?"

"I don't know," she said uncertainly. "I have to think it over."

"There's nothing to think over." Uncle Georges spoke with an air of finality. "We'll take the afternoon bus. Your aunt is expecting us."

Uncle Georges was no more inclined to waste time than to waste money. As soon as they had eaten he went down to the cellar to chop wood, the old crates which Paul had lugged in from some of his night excursions but had not found the opportunity to cut up himself.

"A disgrace!" they heard him muttering to himself. "Nothing gets done in a houseful of women and children." Then his voice was drowned in the steady sound of the ax.

"What do you think, Paul?" his mother asked anxiously.

"I wish we could keep the children here," Paul said wistfully. "It won't be the same without them."

"I do too." His mother sighed. "But Uncle's right. We're not feeding them properly. With all the sickness this winter, it would be wise to send them away. We'll hope it won't be for long."

So it was decided. A few hours later, Mitzi, dressed in her best, and Emile, carrying a package of clean underthings, were put on the bus with Uncle Georges. There was a brief scene when Mitzi screamed that she would not leave, but finally the promise of a visit to a farm with live cows and pigs quieted her down. Madame La Coque and Paul stood by the bus window, while Mitzi, sitting on

Emile's lap, started to see how many kisses she could blow them. The bus moved off before they realized it.

A meeting of the Club of Young Patriots was scheduled at the Chamber of the Underground that evening. Paul had a feeling of proprietorship about their hideout and always liked to get there early to straighten things up. As he scrambled through the tunnel, he spied a ray of light ahead. Evidently he was not the first after all! A surprise was waiting for him.

On the table was a miner's lamp and next to it sat Felix, calmly eating the last of their cans of corned beef.

"Good evening, Paul."

"Felix!" exclaimed Paul in astonishment.

"I ask pardon for arriving without an invitation," said Felix. "It was a case of necessity. All the gendarmes and Germans in Moyelle are looking for me." Briefly, he explained.

"How long have you known about the Chamber?" Paul asked.

"Since the beginning," Felix informed him, smiling.

It was Felix then, Paul realized. It was Felix who had become the leader of the Moyelle Patriots after his father's arrest. Felix, with whom he worked every day at the mines!

Roland, Carlo and Gaston showed up shortly. They were astonished, pleased, and flattered too, that the older man had come to them. The regular business of their meeting was postponed as they gathered around him. He took this occasion to tell them what was happening in other parts of the country.

At first it was isolated groups like theirs, pitifully few and far between, who protested Nazi occupation, Felix explained. At first it had seemed to the majority of the

French that nothing could be done, that the Nazis were as indomitable as they claimed. But the Nazi schedule had broken down. They had never succeeded in invading England. Now America was in the war. The campaign in Russia was proving costly. It was just a question of time—time and the efforts of all of them—until they were free again.

As the Resistance grew stronger, the Nazis increased their vigilance, their reprisals, and their brutality. The cloak of goodwill with which they had masked their arrival was gone now, baring their reign of terror.

From Felix, the boys learned of the twenty-seven Patriots at Châteaubriant who had been shot as hostages in revenge for the killing of one German officer. He told them of five Parisian students, not much older than themselves, who had protested the dismissal of a Jewish professor; all five had been arrested, tortured, shot. He gave them their first news of Oradour, a little town not far from Limoges. Because of a rumor that the town was harboring "terrorists," the Germans had shot the male population, shut up the women and children in the church and set fire to it, then burned the town to the ground. "Oradour will live forever, a memorial of man's inhumanity to man."

He told them about the French Maquis. "The word 'Maquis' originally applied to certain wild land in Corsica covered with low plants and bushes; later it was given to the outlaws from society who hid there. The French Maquis are guerrilla fighters, who live in the mountains or forests. Often they go barefoot, but they carry arms, seized from German army posts or dropped by parachute by the Allies. Since my usefulness in Moyelle is ended, I will likely join up with them now."

The boys listened avidly and would have let him go on talking all night, but he advised them to go on home and sleep. "Sleep is a most precious thing, my boys. You must learn to take it in large doses or small ones, whenever you can."

Before he left, Felix asked Paul to tell his contact—he did not mention Lucette by name—where he was. He also gave him the thousand-franc note to pass on to her for the Moyelle Patriots.

"You will stay here tonight, Felix?" Roland asked.

Felix nodded. "With your permission. It's the safest place I know of."

"I wish it were more comfortable, monsieur," said Gaston regretfully. "If only we had known that you were coming . . ."

"Next time I'll send you a telegram," Felix promised, his eyes twinkling. "Now, if you'll excuse me . . ." He stretched out on one of the cots, pulled the blanket over him, and seemed to be asleep even before they left.

As usual, the boys climbed out of the dugout one by one at several-minute intervals, a precautionary measure. Paul, as he always did, brought up the rear. As he started out, he had the impression that someone or something was moving in the trees. That their hideout might be discovered was always in the back of their minds. Should they once be found out, the harm could not be undone.

Paul's first thought was to alert the others to his suspicion. Then he realized this would be foolish. If there was an intruder, it would be almost impossible to catch him in the dark. On the other hand, if he thought himself unobserved, he might well fall in a trap.

Not until he reached the fence did he give their pre-arranged signal of danger, the whistle of a mockingbird. The other boys soon slipped out of the trees and gathered around him.

"Is something wrong, Paul?"

"We must go back." He told them what he thought he had seen.

Cautiously they retraced their steps to the dugout. The shrubbery which usually covered it had been thrust aside! Soundlessly as cats, they crawled along the tunnel to the Chamber.

Felix was standing next to the table. A man, with his back to the boys, was holding a gun on him.

"I figured those kids would know where you were," he was saying in a voice that Paul quickly recognized. "I followed them. There's no use trying to escape. Alive or dead, there's a price on your head, but it's ten thousand francs alive and only five thousand dead. I don't want to pull the trigger unless I have to."

"A gun makes a man mighty brave, doesn't it, Gustave?" Felix spoke calmly.

"Put up your hands!"

"I don't believe I will. You are not one to throw away five thousand francs so easily."

"No matter. Get moving. Remember as you go through the tunnel that I'm right behind you with this gun."

Felix stood where he was. "What's your hurry? I'd like to talk to you."

"About what?"

"About yourself. I'd like to know just what goes on in a man's head when he decides to sell a fellow worker for ten thousand francs—or even for five thousand."

"A fellow worker!" Gustave spit. "You and the other men, you've always treated me like dirt. Everything's changed now. I'm important. I can get any of you I want sent to jail. Or killed."

Felix looked at him pityingly. "Why don't you be honest with yourself, Gustave? If the men didn't like or trust you even before the war, they had their reasons. Did you really think we wouldn't find out about those trumped-up tales you used to take to the foreman?"

"And if I did?" Gustave asked defiantly. "A man has to look after himself. You think the men all love you. Well, they aren't going to love what the Germans leave of you. . . ."

"Now . . ." whispered Paul.

He sneaked up and with a blow knocked the gun from Gustave's hand. It went off, the bullet ricocheting harmlessly against the wall. As their unwanted visitor turned, Roland tripped him. In a second they had him pinned down.

"Felix," called Roland, "there's a rope beneath the table."

Soon they had Gustave trussed up like a chicken. Beyond speech, he glared at them and sputtered.

"Let him spend the night with me," said Felix with a shrug. "He won't be much company but I don't mind. Sorry you had to miss your sleep again, my boys. Once the Liberation comes, we'll all sleep for a month."

All the way to town the other boys chattered exuberantly about their prisoner-of-war. Only Paul remained silent. His first feeling of triumph at the capture of Gustave had passed. They had a prisoner, but what next? In all of France, there was no prison for traitors. He tried to tell himself that it was not his problem. Felix would know what to do with him. In his heart, he realized, with a sense of dread, that there was only one way that Felix, or anyone else, could solve that problem.

CHAPTER 9

NOT TOO SOON NOR TOO LATE

There were six men in the office on the second floor of the *gendarmerie*. One was Kommandant Schmidt, seated behind a large desk. On either side of him two muscular German adjutants with empty, brutalized faces stood at attention. By the door were two French gendarmes.

The sixth person was an old man with long handlebar mustaches, dressed in shabby trousers and jacket. He was seated on a straight chair in front of the Kommandant's desk, his hands tied behind him to the rungs of the chair. His head was lopped slightly to the side and there was no expression in his vacant eyes.

"Now, Robert, we not want to hurt you," the Kommandant was saying. "You just tell us what we ask and nothing happen to you. You hear me?"

The old man made no sign of either hearing or understanding.

"Who were the terrorists who rob Town Hall the other night?" the Kommandant demanded.

Still no sound from the prisoner.

"Who told you let them in? What door they use?"

Old Robert remained both motionless and silent.

"You are making mistake to behave so stubbornly," said the Kommandant in an oily voice. "A bad mistake. You force us refresh your memory." He signaled one of the adjutants. "Refresh his memory."

The adjutant stepped forward, raised his right arm, struck the prisoner a slashing blow in the mouth. Old Robert groaned with pain.

The Kommandant nodded approval. "You see? You are not dumb, Robert. Now, maybe you remember. Who were the terrorists?"

Robert's head sunk down on his chest. He gave no more evidence of hearing the German than before.

"You like another memory refresher?"

No answer.

The Kommandant nodded to the second adjutant. "See what you can do."

The second blow fell on the side of Robert's head. Again he moaned.

"You vant more?" When Robert said nothing, the Kommandant jumped up from his desk. "Vat sort of foolishness is this? I make him talk." He grabbed his revolver by the barrel and held it above the prisoner, as though to bring the butt crashing down on his skull. "For last time. Who were the terrorists?"

Seemingly with a tremendous effort the old man raised up his head. Blood was trickling from his mouth and forehead and he had the look of a tortured animal. He stared directly at the Kommandant, at his livid red face, his ponderous body, the eagle and swastika emblem on his epaulets. Then he spoke.

"You are Death," he said. "You have come for me at last." And he actually smiled.

The Kommandant lowered his arm. The revolver went clammering to the floor. "A madman! A lunatic!" He glared at the others in the room.

One of the gendarmes—the same who had previously taken Robert home—stepped forward. "It is as I explained, Monsieur le Kommandant. The man is not normal. He is, I might say, simple in the head, the result of an accident in the mines. He has been like this for many years."

"So! You let me waste my time on an idiot?" shouted the Kommandant furiously, ignoring or forgetting that when the gendarmes had brought Robert in, they had said questioning him would be useless. "Take him away. Get him out of my sight."

Silently the adjutants released the cords that bound the prisoner's arms. The two gendarmes led him out of the room.

On the same morning that old Robert made his curious remark to Kommandant Schmidt, his sister paid a call on Madame La Coque, Paul's mother. She wore a scarf tied over her head as the miners' wives did, rather than a hat, and like any neighbor she went around to the back and knocked at the kitchen door.

"Come in!" called Madame La Coque, who was having coffee with Hélène Michel. "Why, Mademoiselle Ricard, how nice to see you." She rose and offered her a chair. "Won't you join us?"

"With pleasure." The schoolteacher accepted the chair. "But no coffee, madame. It doesn't agree with me." Her voice was friendly and warm, with no trace of her burning anxiety about her brother. "*Bonjour,* Madame Michel. I'm so glad you are here. I did want to see both of you."

"*Bonjour,* mademoiselle." Roland's mother shook hands with her. "I come often to visit with Annette because both our husbands were sent away together and with her I can talk openly. You should know that the last we heard they were in Holland. But then their postcards stopped coming and our letters have been returned, marked 'Not here.'" She spoke with composure, showing none of her former hysteria. Sorrow had taught her fortitude.

"It is about your husbands I have come," announced the visitor. "I have news of them."

The other two women went white. "Tell us quickly," Madame La Coque murmured weakly.

"I have just received a letter from a friend in the Auvergne." Mademoiselle Ricard did not explain that she had never met this "friend" and that his message had come to her through clandestine channels. "He was a prisoner in Germany but was fortunately released. In camp he knew both Monsieur La Coque and Monsieur Michel. He promised them to let you know that they were alive and as well as could be expected."

"They are in a concentration camp?" cried Madame La Coque. Information about the fearful conditions of such camps had seeped through to Moyelle.

Mademoiselle Ricard nodded gravely. "The camp at Oranienburg, which is about nineteen miles from Berlin. It is not the worst, but neither is it good. I felt you would want to know the truth. Many do die in these camps but my friend wrote that most of the casualties occur in the first weeks. Those with the stamina to survive through that period have a good chance."

"Our husbands are well? Your friend said that?" Madame La Coque clung to that one comforting statement.

"Yes. As well as can be expected. That is what he said. I wish I could tell you more but that is all I know." She rose. "You must excuse me now. I have some other calls to make."

Madame La Coque went to the door with her. "I am deeply grateful to you, mademoiselle. Particularly since I know you have trouble of your own. May I ask if you have news of Monsieur Robert?"

The schoolteacher shook her head. "None. They still will not let me see him."

"I do sympathize with you."

"Thank you, my dear. We are in the same boat now, are we not?" She reached up and kissed the miner's wife on both cheeks, in the fashion of the country.

Paul's mother told him the news about his father while he was having dinner, a couple of hours later.

Paul's face brightened. Though he too had heard bad things about concentration camps, he could not really believe them. "Mother, I know he'll come back."

"I try to tell myself that too, Paul. But it has been over six months now. Sometimes it seems to me I cannot endure another twenty-four hours of waiting."

It was so unusual for her to utter any word of complaint that Paul looked up sharply. She was standing by the stove, frying his potatoes in the rancid grease which was all they had, her head half turned from him. It suddenly struck him how much she had changed since his father's arrest. She had always been slender, but now her faded housedress hung on her far too loosely. Her dark hair had lost its luster and her cheeks were hollow and sunken.

"My poor mother!" Impulsively he jumped up and embraced her. "You must take better care of yourself. We must fatten you up before Father comes back."

"Nonsense," she scoffed, pushing him away. "Your father doesn't like fat women. Finish your dinner. After you eat, you ought to go see Mademoiselle Ricard. She must be lonely without her brother. I feel so sorry for her. How dreadful for a woman not to have a husband and children!"

What a curious thing for his mother to say! Here she was, worn to the bone looking after him, torn to bits because she had let Mitzi and Emile go stay with their uncle, and suffering unspeakable torments about the fate of her husband. Yet she was full of pity for a woman who had only a brother to worry about.

"I'll pay her a visit after I bring home the bread," Paul promised.

"Would you like me to get it so you can take a nap first?"

"No, Mother, I don't mind. You get some rest."

He could not tell her that it was urgent he go to the Cooperative that afternoon—to deliver Felix's message to Lucette.

For the first time Lucette was late. Paul already had his bread and was dawdling around outside the Cooperative when she came running up.

"Oh, Paul," she cried, her face anguished. "Something terrible has happened. One of our best people has disappeared. I've seen his wife. She knows nothing. Paul, if they make him talk—and mind you, I don't think they can—it would mean the end of everything. But they will try— they will try every trick in their foul books. I feel as if it were happening to me, as if I were being torn limb from limb. . . ."

Luckily, no one was near enough to hear her outburst, but several people down the street turned and stared curiously.

"Calm yourself, Lucette." Paul spoke in a masterful

tone. "You should know better than to make a spectacle of yourself." He seized her arm and marched her away from the Cooperative.

"Yes, Paul," Lucette said. Obediently, she put on a set smile. "Is that better?"

"A little." Paul smiled back at her, with the difference that his smile was genuine. "Now you can go tell Madame Virel that her husband is safe and sound." He pressed the one-thousand-franc note into her hand. "And he says you will know what to do with this." Briefly, he told about Felix's arrival at the Chamber of the Underground the night before.

"Paul, how could you wait so long to let us know?" Lucette pouted, most unreasonably since she had ordered him never to come to her home. "You should have told me sooner."

Trust Lucette not to admit that even she might have a moment of weakness.

When Paul reached home with his bread, his mother was standing at the kitchen table, cutting out a pattern for a dress for the wife of the architect.

"I told you to rest, Mother. Can't you ever stop working?"

"You want me to be a fine lady, sitting with my hands crossed all day long?" His mother looked up with a rueful smile. "Work keeps me from thinking. The less I think these days, the better off I am."

"I guess nothing will change you." He stood before her, hesitant.

"What is it, Paul?"

"I wondered if you could spare some of our bread," he blurted out. "It's for a friend—who won't eat unless I can bring him something."

"But of course, Paul." His mother took the bread from him and cut several slices. "Luckily, we have a little butter left to spread on it. You'll find a hard-boiled egg in the cupboard. And there's some coffee left over from dinner. Why don't you fill your thermos bottle? Bad as it is, it's better than nothing."

Not a single question as to where this precious food was going! Paul stared in amazed gratitude. The more he saw of women, the less he understood them.

It was still daylight, too soon to risk going to the Chamber with Felix's lunch. As Paul had promised his mother, he stopped to see Mademoiselle Ricard. He found her distraught but hospitable as always.

"It was sweet of you to come, Paul. Your tea will be ready in a moment."

"About Monsieur Robert," Paul burst out. "Isn't there something we can do? What about a raid on the *gendarmerie?* I'm sure there are enough of us to carry it off successfully."

"No, Paul." She shook her head firmly. "Even if it worked, what could we do with him? If he came home, they'd only come get him again. And he can't take care of himself anywhere else. I've thought it over. There's nothing to do but wait. . . ."

She had barely spoken when the door opened and her brother shuffled in. His face was swollen and bruised but otherwise he seemed unharmed.

"Robert, is it really you?" His sister darted over to him. "Oh, your poor face! What have they done to you?" She took him by the arm and helped him to his chaise longue. "Sit down, my brother. Rest yourself. You're safe now. You're with me. Get some water, Paul. I must see how badly he is hurt. There, there, Robert. You must be

hungry. I'll fix you some tea. Then we'll eat." All this
came out in a series of staccato phrases, very unlike
Mademoiselle Ricard's usual careful speech.

Old Robert sank into the chaise longue with an air of
uncertainty. Paul fetched some warm water in a bowl and
held it while the schoolteacher bathed her brother's face.
"Oh, Robert," she murmured, letting out little moans of
personal pain at his cuts and bruises. "The brutes! The
brutes!"

Why, she loves him, thought Paul wonderingly. In her
way she loves him as much as Mother loves me.

"Do you feel better now, monsieur?" he asked politely.

"Yes, yes." The old man's glance wandered around the
room. "Soon it will be too late."

Obviously, he lived in a world of his own fantasies where
no one else could enter. And yet—his sister had told Paul
that he had occasional lucid spells and he was certainly able
to obey the simple orders of Madame Josephine at the
Town Hall. Could the Kommandant have found out something from him? Paul felt he must try to find out.

When Mademoiselle Ricard went into the kitchen, he
knelt beside the old man.

"Monsieur," he pleaded softly. "I want you to tell me
what happened at the *gendarmerie*. What they asked you
and what you said to them."

He looked at Paul blankly. "Soon it will be too late."

"Try to remember," Paul insisted. "It is important. For
your sister, for all of us. Did they ask you who tied up old
Nicolas?"

"Yes, yes," he said. "Old Nicolas. The terrorists"—a word
he had obviously picked up from the Kommandant—"the
terrorists tied him up like a chicken to be roasted in the
oven." He giggled childishly.

Paul stirred with impatience. He was getting nowhere. Well, he would make one last attempt.

"Did they ask you who tied up old Nicolas, monsieur?" he repeated.

"Yes, yes." Robert turned and stared at him. "They asked me. I wouldn't tell them. Do you want to know why?"

"I do very much." Paul tried to tone down his excitement, so as not to frighten the old man.

"Promise you won't tell?"

"I promise."

"My room," Robert whispered. "They came out of my room. Beneath the stove. I didn't want him to know about my room. He would have said I couldn't go there and smoke my pipe. He would have scolded me and told Madame Josephine."

The faint smell of tobacco the first time Paul and Roland entered the brick room beneath the Town Hall! Suddenly Paul understood.

"Paul!" Mademoiselle Ricard was standing in the doorway holding her tea tray. "What is he saying to you?"

"It's all right, mademoiselle," Paul said, rising. "Monsieur Robert told the Kommandant nothing."

"But of course he didn't!" There was a slightly shocked expression on her face. "He is my brother."

Paul went alone to the Chamber that evening. No one could be sure that Gustave had been alone when he followed them the night before. If he hadn't, the place might still be watched. The other boys had agreed that Paul, with his unusually keen eyesight and sharp ears, would have the best chance to elude the watchers. But the woods were silent and empty, so far as Paul could discover. He was as certain as he could be that no one saw him.

Felix was sitting alone at the table. There was no sign of their prisoner.

"Where is he?" Paul asked, almost dreading the answer.

"I have something to tell you, Paul," Felix said slowly. "Gustave has committed suicide."

"Suicide? After the way we trussed him up? How could he?"

"To tell the truth it was not last night that he did it," Felix went on. "He committed suicide a long time ago—when he first decided he liked money better than honor."

"And you finished the job for him." His voice broke. Gustave, even though he despised him, was someone he knew, not just an abstract enemy. "Oh, Felix!"

"I know." Felix rose and put his arm around his shoulders. "I did not enjoy being both judge and jury, Paul, but I had no choice. We could not keep him here and we could not set him free. I buried him beside Fritz. Of the two, Fritz was certainly the better man. He was only a soldier doing his duty, but Gustave betrayed his own—and that is a different matter. We must try not to think about it. Now tell me what has happened."

Paul told him, first about his father, then about Robert's return from the *gendarmerie*.

"Two pieces of good news in one day. That's splendid."

"And Mother sent you some bread and an egg and some coffee," Paul added.

"More good news." Felix smiled down on him. "I'll admit I'm a mite hungry."

Just then Paul heard a light noise in the tunnel. "Felix! Someone's coming!" Had he been less observant than he thought when he crossed the woods? He would never forgive himself if now . . .

Felix seized Gustave's hunting gun. Footsteps approached, lightly and uncertainly.

"Don't shoot, Felix. It's I. Lucette."

She stepped into the Chamber as Felix lowered the gun.

"So this is your famous hideout. Well, I must say I don't think much of it. I've never seen a gloomier spot in all my life." There was no trace of the panic-stricken young girl whom Paul had chastised earlier in the day.

"What are you doing here, Lucette?" he demanded roughly.

She ignored him. "Felix, I've brought you a suit of clothes. They belonged to my father." She bit her lips to force away her emotion. "There's some money in small notes in the pocket. Don't argue about it, you'll need it. The orders are for you to leave here tonight. You will stay on a farm temporarily, and after that we'll find a way to get you out of Pas de Calais. It's going to be hard to be without you, Felix. Do change your clothes and let's get out of here. Paul, you don't need to worry about my visiting you often. I can think of more cheerful places to pass my time."

"You're quite a girl, little Lucette," Felix said with a grin. "Take care of Paul and his pals while I'm gone. Make sure they don't decide to blitzkrieg the Nazis all on their own."

After Felix had put on the suit that had once belonged to Monsieur Du Bois, the three of them walked to the road together. Paul stepped aside, while Lucette gave Felix directions to get to the farm. That was the first rule of the Resistants, that no one should know more than he needed to know. Then Felix kissed Lucette on both cheeks, shook hands warmly with Paul, and with a wave of his hand was off toward Vimy.

"Good luck," Paul whispered softly after him. He felt his throat tighten. It was going to be lonesome without Felix.

"When do you think it will be over?" Paul asked Lucette

as they walked back to Moyelle. "When do you think we'll be rid of the Nazis?"

"Your guess is as good as mine," she said. "Like all tyrants, I would say that Hitler has bitten off more than he can chew."

"With America on our side, it shouldn't take long."

She shook her head. "The Germans are still strong. Remember they have slave labor from nearly all Europe—Poland, Denmark, Belgium, Holland, Czechoslovakia, Norway, and from our own people. My feeling is that there will be a lot of misery and suffering before the end comes. But we can't stop for that. We have to go on doing our job, no matter how long it takes."

Lucette might have her moments of weakness, like all women, but Felix was right when he said she was quite a girl. Only a year older than himself and she talked politics like a man. And coming out here alone at night! Most females would have been frightened out of their wits. Paul kept such thoughts to himself. There was no use telling Lucette he admired her.

"How's your mother?" he asked abruptly.

"Not too well," confided Lucette. "With her high blood pressure, the work in the fields is not good for her."

"Have they bothered her any more about your father?"

"Every so often they send someone around—Germans or gendarmes. She always sticks to the same story—that she learned about my father's accident in a dream."

"It wasn't a dream?"

"Of course not. I can tell you, now that it doesn't matter any more. It was Felix who let her know about my father."

It had been a very remarkable day, Paul reflected as he crept into bed. Because it had also been a very exhausting day, in two minutes he was sound asleep.

CHAPTER 10

THE "LAMENTABLE INCIDENTS"

"One. Two. Three. Four." Master Varenne's stentorian tones coincided with a metallic clang, as his apprentice-students, standing at their benches, hammered upright iron bars held in position by a vise.

"Hammer with your right hand first," the Master chanted. "Now switch to your left. One. Two. Three. Four. Gaston, not so awkward. Easily now. So! Carlo, pay attention! A good railroad man must be as skillful with his left hand as with his right. We all want to be good railroad men, don't we, boys?"

"Yes, monsieur," his students chorused dutifully.

A funny-looking duck, the Master, Gaston was thinking, with the two bright red spots on his cheeks and the fringe of black curly hair making a neat circle around the bald cone of the top of his head. Before the war they had often played practical jokes on him. Now they treated him with the greatest care, fearful lest the German directors of the railroads should take him away and substitute a Vichy man.

Master Varenne, old-fashioned and stodgy as he was, was a loyal Frenchman and they all knew it.

Hitting iron bars with hammers . . . filing iron cubes to exact dimensions . . . learning every part of the locomotive and how it functioned—all went into the training that would make the youths into motormen, firemen, trackmen. One more year and Gaston and Carlo would be finished with their apprenticeship and would be full-fledged railroad men on full salary. That, at least, was something to look forward to.

It was April, 1944, and France had been occupied by the Nazis nearly four years. The long-awaited Second Front, the invasion of the Continent by the Allies, was still in the future, awaited with painful anxiety. In the last two years, misfortune had struck the homes of both boys. Their fathers, who were part of the Resistance group within the railroads, had been denounced by a traitor. Gaston's father had fled and was now in hiding, none of his family knew where. Carlo's had been arrested by the French police, working under German orders, and was imprisoned at Doullens, in the Somme, about thirty miles from Moyelle. Once a week Carlo or his Italian mother made the long trip on bicycle, to bring him food packages. Occasionally they were permitted to talk with him but more often they had to leave their packages with the guards, whom they suspected of confiscating them for their own use.

"Enough!" cried the Master suddenly. "Put away your tools, boys. Before you leave I have two most lamentable incidents to relate."

His students settled to rapt attention.

"A few nights ago," the Master began, "I don't recall the exact date—I believe it was Thursday but it might have been Wednesday—my memory is sometimes a bit faulty, my boys, you must pardon an old man. Well then, on Wednesday or Thursday night, a train carrying German troops, our guests for the duration, ran off the track on a bridge not far from Lens. By a remarkable coincidence, it so happened that another train, filled with produce donated to our German neighbors by the farmers of France, was steaming along the underpass just as the first train collapsed." He illustrated the event with copious gestures. "Wasn't that a tragic thing, my boys? Two train-loads of cargo lost forever—one human, one pig!"

He took off his spectacles and wiped them, seeming to rid them of invisible tears. Obligingly his students assumed masks of great dismay. They knew better than to betray their inner jubilation. There were spies everywhere.

Nearly every day the Master had a "lamentable incident" to tell them. Frequently it had to do with derailed trains. (The Patriots no longer used dynamite for this purpose but simply loosened or detached a rail, a much simpler and equally effective method.) There were other things.

A locomotive boiler exploded because of an undetected leak; repairing it took a full week. Crates of champagne, "a gift of appreciation from the grateful French," arrived in Germany, every bottle broken. A cargo of wheat was also sent as "a present to the German people," but some-how the sacks were ripped and "wheat dribbled from here to the Fatherland." Then there was the train scheduled to go to Germany but for which the instructions were unac-countably switched. "Believe me or not, boys, the com-pany had a devil of a time finding out where that train went. A week later it showed up in Bordeaux."

Every time he thought of that train wandering lost all over the south of France, Gaston had to laugh. The memory of it returned inopportunely in class this day, and

he collapsed into a coughing fit which even Carlo's sound
blow between his shoulder blades failed to stop.

The Master fixed him with a cold stare. "When Monsieur Gaston recovers from his disorder, I have another
lamentable incident to relate."

Gaston calmed down at once.

"Not only in the railroads do such things occur," continued the Master. "I tell you now about The Great Mine
Robbery. Yes, boys, a robbery. A few nights ago one of
those gallant German sentinels who patrol the mines was
knocked unconscious by a band of gangsters, one of whom
changed clothes with their victim. His fellow sentinels,
whose eyesight was apparently none too good, suspected
nothing amiss, and the masquerader was able to let his con-
spirators in through the gate. After taking the French
guards hostages, they succeeded in escaping with a cache
of eight hundred pounds of dynamite!"

He took off his spectacles and wiped them again.

"It may be purely coincidental," he concluded, "that
only two days later an automobile plant near Paris, where
our German friends now build those tanks and other vehicles with which they strive to keep peace in Europe, was
blown up. By luck no French worker was on duty when it
happened."

Carlo and Gaston stared straight ahead, not daring to ex-
change glances. They both knew all about "The Great
Mine Robbery." The suggestion for it had come from
Paul, who had not forgotten what Felix had said so long before about the dynamite cache on the seventh level. The
two railroad apprentices had acted as lookouts for the
trucks sent from a neighboring town to pick up the loot,
while Roland and Paul, because of their familiarity with
the mines, had gone along with the older men on the raid.

But they had not heard before of the explosion in the con-verted automobile plant near Paris.

"That is all for today," said the Master. "Now rise and let us sing together 'The Future is Yours.' "

Clear and strong, the young voices rang out with the words of the song which many generations of apprentices had sung before them:

> "Young apprentices are we,
>   Starting on the road of life.
>   Gay and strong and full of hope,
>   Unafraid of coming strife."

"Class is dismissed," called the Master. His students had scattered before the words were out of his mouth.

Gaston and Carlo walked out together.

"I feel strange," Carlo said, as they headed for their homes, between the rows of pretty stucco cottages of the Cité des Cheminots. "When I think of it. Our dynamite! Because of it who knows how many German tanks put out of commission! Who knows how many Allied lives saved!"

Gaston nodded contentedly. "At least we've graduated from selling butterflies at five francs each. As Master Varenne pointed out, The Great Mine Robbery was done by gangsters."

"Don't say that." Carlo's voice was low and intense. "We're not gangsters. The Nazis are the gangsters. We must not forget that."

"What's the matter with you?" Gaston demanded, puz-zled. "You don't have to lecture me. You know very well how I feel about the Nazis."

"I know." Carlo hesitated. "I was really lecturing myself. Sometimes it seems to me we're so used to breaking laws that we'll have a fearful time after the war learning to obey them."

"That's the least of my worries." Gaston started to yawn but in the midst of it, he stopped, his mouth hanging open. "Do you see what I see?"

Coming toward them were the Vichy Mayor and Kommandant Schmidt, escorted by his German adjutants, on foot for some reason, and no doubt on their way to discuss more "lamentable incidents" with the railroad directors. The Mayor had gained a good deal of weight since coming to Moyelle, a source of bitter jibes from the towns-people, suffering from the effects of four years of malnutrition.

"Now's our chance," whispered Gaston. He and Carlo darted into an alley, hiding behind a stack of bricks. As the officials passed them, they burst out into a chant:

> "The Mayor of Moyelle
> Has made a Proclamation
> To the Population;
> Henceforth no one is to eat dry bread!
>
> "Everybody
> Young and old, men and women
> From this day forth
> Is hereby ordered
> To dunk their bread in water!"

They stayed where they were just long enough to catch a glimpse of the Mayor's outraged face, then turned and ran down the alley, counting on the fact that to adults all young boys at a distance look alike. Unfortunately, at the end of the alley they ran plunk into two French gendarmes.

The Mayor was shouting and the Kommandant was bellowing, as the gendarmes dragged the resisting youths back with them.

"So!" ejaculated the red-faced Kommandant. "You play joke on your Mayor. Very funny. Maybe you think this is funny." He tweaked each in turn by the ear. The boys winced.

"Vat you want done with them, Mayor? Shall I lock them up?"

"No, no," stammered the Mayor. "I don't want any trouble."

"Trouble? All the time you have trouble here because you don't want trouble. I say put them in a cell. Then see if they want to make jokes, *hein?*"

"No, no," repeated the Mayor in embarrassment. "I feel sure they meant no harm."

"You know vat you are, Mayor?" demanded the Kommandant wrathfully. "You are not a man. You are a dummy. No one respect you because you are a dummy. You not know how to handle people. Force! That's all they understand."

"But, my Kommandant," pleaded the Mayor. "If you lock up young boys only because they make a joke against me, everybody in town will laugh. Let them go, I beg of you. You won't do it again, will you, boys?"

"No, monsieur," Gaston promised.

"You see, Kommandant? They are sorry."

"Very well," snapped the German officer. "You can go. But I never forget faces. Next time you not get off so easy."

Once out of sight, the boys breathed deeply.

"That was a foolish idea of mine," Gaston admitted sheepishly. "We're not children any more. We should never have risked getting caught for such a bagatelle."

"No harm done," said Carlo cheerfully. "We got away, didn't we?"

"By a miracle. But we made ourselves known to the enemy—which is the very thing not to do."

Carlo kicked a small stone in the road. "I'm not sorry. It was fun."

Fun was a luxury in which they had little chance to indulge since the foundation of the Club of Young Patriots. Like Felix, they had learned to snatch sleep when they could, a few minutes, or a few seconds, at a time. They were all thin as broomsticks, nor had they grown much in height—which was an advantage. The German patrol, which occasionally stopped them when they bicycled out in the country and a few times caught them out after curfew, dismissed them as youngsters though they were now approaching manhood and, with occasional lapses, were mature beyond their years. They could pride themselves that they had earned the right to consider themselves men. Were they not part of the Resistance, the movement that had begun slowly in sporadic outbursts here and there, and which now, with the imminence of the Second Front, was spreading with gathering momentum in every corner of France?

They were nearing their homes, walking in the middle of the road as they always did, when a bicycle swerved from around the corner, almost bumping into them.

"Watch where you're going!" called Gaston, and then stopped short, seeing that the rider was Lucette.

She dismounted serenely.

"Hello. How nice to see you. How have you been?" She lowered her voice. "I did not mean to run you down but I was afraid I was going to miss you. You are to be at the Chamber tonight at eight. Paul and Roland will be there."

"But I thought there were to be no more meetings for a while," Gaston said in surprise. "That's what Jean-Luc said." Jean-Luc was the young miner who had taken over the leadership of the Moyelle Patriots now that nearly all the older men, the first Resistants, were gone. "He said we were to lay low until the furor over the dynamite raid died down."

"I know. But something came up. You boys were chosen because you're less under surveillance than the older men. I've got to get on home now." She sprang gracefully on her bicycle and waved them good-bye with the bright smile she used before strangers."

"One thing about Lucette," Carlo commented wryly. "She never wastes time."

Many changes had been made in the Chamber of the Underground the last two years. Not infrequently, men sought by the Nazis hid out there for a few days. Sometimes men wounded in local skirmishes were brought in. A doctor sympathizer, whom they knew as Doctor Pinot, had joined their ranks. He was a mild scholarly man with rimmed glasses and a hesitant manner, but he had courage and would arrive at the Chamber on short notice at any hour of the night. To him the boys had turned over the suitcase of medical equipment, for his own use or to pass on to other Resistance doctors.

For their visitors, they now had a stock of tinned biscuit, sardines, and other foods, as well as a limited supply of bottles of mineral water and wine. Mademoiselle Ricard's Sterno permitted them to heat coffee or make a cup of tea. They had a radio on which they could listen to broadcasts from London, and a mimeograph machine on which they now and again ran off leaflets for the older Resistants.

A cache of ammunition was now hidden in the inside

tunnel, and as a special precaution, they had dug a second tunnel, leading from the cache to the cellar of a bombed-out house in the fields, with the entrance carefully concealed and known only to a select few.

There was a strong door to close off the Chamber of the Underground from the dugout entrance in the woods. The door to the little room beneath the Town Hall had been repaired too, and this was always kept locked. Their hideout had become a real fortress!

Practically all their visitors, whether they stayed a few hours or a few days, had contributed to the improvements, and one, an electrician, had fitted up a special device to be used only in case of great emergency.

Before he left, the electrician had given the boys a warning. "Sooner or later," he said, "some of the persons you harbor here are going to be captured by the Nazis. Sooner or later, one of these may be forced to talk. You must be prepared for everything."

Though they realized the logic behind his warning, in their hearts they could not accept it. For them, the Chamber seemed to have a charmed existence. Only here did they feel safe from the danger they lived with day and night, danger that someone would betray them, danger that they might be caught in the midst of some "illegal" activity.

It seemed strange, after all the varied pattern of company, that the four charter members of the Club should find themselves alone on that spring night. Paul, who had arrived first, had brought a stencil which Lucette had given him. Their assignment was to make a thousand mimeographed copies.

"What's in the stencil, Paul?"

He shook his head. "I know no more about it than you do."

The mimeograph machine was an old one, and they had

to turn it slowly, taking out each sheet and drying it separately. They were all curious.

"Read it," suggested Paul. "Read it aloud, Roland, while we're working."

"Attention, People of Moyelle," he began with a theatrical flourish. "Tonight the Allies are planning to bomb the railroad depot!"

Carlo let out a whoop of delight. "It's come at last! The prelude to the Second Front."

"The German war machine is cracking," Roland read on. "Africa is cleared of Axis forces. Italy has surrendered. Massive air raids of the RAF have demolished Lübeck, a major Baltic outlet for Nazi supplies, and have reduced to ashes Rostock, the site of the Nazi Heinkel large aircraft. Every day from airfields all over England bombers roar eastward to converge over one industrial center after another. The populace of the Ruhr has fled. . . ."

The leaflet ended on a somber note. Because of the projected bombing of the depot, all citizens of Moyelle were advised to evacuate their homes and leave town.

"But why?" demanded Carlo. "Why, if they're only going to bomb the depot, should everyone get out?"

"I suppose it's difficult to bomb accurately from the height of the planes," Paul suggested. "I suppose a bomb might land somewhere beyond the depot." He could not guess what an understatement he had uttered.

"Even so," Roland said, "how can people leave town? Where would they go and with what? No one has any money to travel these days—except the collaborators and the black marketeers."

"I'm not going," Gaston announced. "I want to look out my window and see the bombs falling on the locomotives. I wouldn't miss it for anything."

"Nor I." Carlo spoke with fierce intensity. "It's nearly

over now. If we can hold out a little longer, we will be here for the end."

"There's a Verity of La Palice!" scoffed Roland.

Carlo looked blank. "What do you mean?" French as he considered himself, there were still some French sayings he did not know.

La Palice, Paul explained for his benefit, was a French captain of the fifteenth century who was killed in a battle at Pavia. In his honor his soldiers composed a song which ended: "A quarter of an hour before his death, he was still among the living." Ever since, any obvious statement was called a "Verity of La Palice."

"We may be here after the end if we don't get these things run off," commented Roland, returning to the mimeograph machine.

In another hour they had finished. Then they tied up the leaflets in four packages, one for each of them. Paul told them where to take them. Others would do the distribution, and the boys took it for granted that it would be done early in the morning and that the bombing was scheduled for the morrow. In any case, their work was done. They blew out the candles, locked the door, and headed down the tunnel.

"I'm getting so I hate to go home," Gaston said. "The Chamber has become my real home. I'm going to miss it."

"Perhaps we can continue to meet here and talk over old times," suggested Carlo.

"We'll become as much of a bore as my Uncle Joseph," called Roland over his shoulder. "If I've heard his stories about the First World War once, I've heard them a thousand times."

They were talking just as though the fighting were already over, reflected Paul with an odd sense of elation.

They had reached the dugout, which was also shipshape

now. The broken boards had been replaced by a solid trapdoor weighted down by turf and grass. Strangers might
have stomped on top of it, not guessing its existence. Tonight, buoyed up by the knowledge that the Allies were
sending help from the skies, they didn't bother with their
usual precaution of spacing their exit. Carlo, Roland and
Gaston scooted out first, with Paul at their heels.

Then it happened. A guttural voice shouted "Halt!" Out
of the darkness a score or so of uniformed figures emerged.

"Hands up!"

Paul, who was still halfway in the dugout, had just time
to reach down and press a small button. Then he was
prodded to his feet.

"Squad One," an unknown voice barked. "Stay behind
and examine the territory for illegal material. Squad Two
surround the prisoners. Forward." The commands were in
German, of which Paul now knew enough to make their
meaning clear.

Roughly the boys were pushed and shoved on a last
macabre march through the woods and across the fields
they knew so well.

Two trucks were waiting on the road, guarded by more
uniformed Germans. They were hoisted into one of them,
forced into a corner, where the soldiers tied their arms and
feet and piled them on top of each other like so many little
sausages. Then, just as the truck was starting, the noise of
the motor was drowned by an explosion from across the
field and a sudden flare appeared against the sky!

The electrician's scheme had worked! Squad One, which
had stayed behind to "examine the territory for illegal
material," would not see the light of day again. Even at
that moment of triumph and danger, Paul could not help
feeling a pang that he would never in his old age be able to
revisit the Chamber of the Underground.

CHAPTER 11

THE LAST OF THE KOMMANDANT

How tired he was! In the painful glare of the spotlight, Paul struggled desperately to keep his eyes open. The four of them were lined up before the Kommandant's desk in the same office of the *gendarmerie* where Robert Ricard had been examined. They had been there, so it seemed, an eternity.

One after another the Germans had pounded questions at them. There was the violent lieutenant who had threatened them. There was the dapper one who had said coaxingly, "Now, boys, just tell us the truth and you can sleep. You must be sensible. You know you will tell us sooner or later. Why not get it over with?"

Now it was the Kommandant himself, furious at having his rest interrupted. He had recognized Gaston and Carlo at once. "You, again! I knew I should have had you locked up. That fool of a Mayor! You not get off easy this time."

And the questioning had begun all over again.

"Who are the other members of your group?" He was addressing Paul.

"Nobody," said Paul. "We worked alone."

On the desk was a pitcher of ice water from which the Kommandant frequently drank deep gulps. Paul tried not to look at it, nor to think of the dryness of his own throat. On the desk also were their mimeographed leaflets.

"Who is your leader?"

"I am, Monsieur le Kommandant," Paul told him.

"Who wrote the leaflet?"

"I did."

"You lie!" The Kommandant scowled. "Where you get the mimeograph machine?"

"We found it," Paul said wearily.

"Where did you find it?"

"I don't remember, Monsieur le Kommandant."

"You will remember." The Kommandant's high rasping voice grated like sandpaper on a raw wound. "Where you get the stencil?"

"I stole it."

"And the paper too, I suppose?" he asked sarcastically.

"Yes, Monsieur le Kommandant."

He repeated the same questions to the other three boys and they gave the same answers that Paul had given, each claiming to be the leader and solely responsible for the leaflets.

"You think you make fools out of us!" the Kommandant said icily. "You will learn otherwise." This was the same man who, on his first appearance in Moyelle, had struck Paul as a comedy character in a play.

How long would the grilling continue? How long must they stand at attention, the glaring spotlight in their eyes? Would it ever end? Or, as was more likely, was this just a prelude to far worse forms of torture? Paul thought long-ingly of his bed at home, of its clean sheets and soft mattress. If only he could rest just a few moments! At his side Carlo, who with all his patriotic fervor was the least physically strong of them, was swaying on his feet. Surreptitiously, Paul nudged him awake. It was essential they hold out. At least until news of their arrest had reached their comrades and those whose names they knew had time to escape.

"So! The German war machine is cracking?" The Kommandant held one of their leaflets beneath their noses. "You will see how the German war machine cracks—"

Just as he uttered the word "cracks," the sky outside seemed to burst into flame, as though the Teutonic gods of ancient times were providing stage effects for this twentieth-century Nazi. Almost simultaneously, there was a deadening crash.

"Mein Gott! An air raid! The leaflet told the truth!"

Hitler's "superman" was underneath his desk in a flash. The other Germans and the French gendarmes fled. The boys were lifted up in the air and tossed to the floor in a heap, as the whole front of the *gendarmerie* crumbled beneath their eyes.

It was actually only a few seconds later that Paul disentangled his arms and legs and rose shakily to his feet. All around them bombs were falling, one after another. The glaring spotlight was gone, but it was light as day.

"Roland! Carlo! Gaston!" He pulled at their inert bodies.

Carlo slowly emerged from the rubble. There was a gash on his forehead and blood was streaming down his jacket.

"You are hurt, Carlo."

"I don't think so." The Italian-born lad rubbed his forehead and looked dubiously at the blood on his hand. "It's only a surface cut."

Gaston struggled up next, and stretched to find himself whole and in one piece. But Roland did not move. Paul bent over him.

"He's unconscious!" He had to shout to make himself heard above the explosions. "We have to get him to a doctor." In his benumbed state, he forgot that they were allegedly prisoners.

"What's happened to the Kommandant?" asked Gaston.

They stared in amazement. The desk beneath which their persecutor had taken refuge had vanished, replaced by a gaping hole. In the mass of broken boards, bricks and plaster, the light reflected on a gleaming surface, the highly polished Nazi boot, sticking straight up in the air. It was the last they saw of Kommandant Schmidt.

Between them, they carried Roland down the main stairway, or what was left of it. Paul, still in a state of shock, had the weird impression that it was suspended in the air, attached to nothing. For years he would dream about that stairway, against a background of crumbling walls, melting and re-forming beneath his feet.

Once outside the *gendarmerie,* they found themselves in a nightmare of piercing shrieks and crashing buildings and human forms scurrying futilely hither and yon.

"To the schoolhouse," he directed the others.

The cement basement of the brick schoolhouse, on the far side of the Town Square, was the nearest thing to an air shelter the town had to offer. Already several wounded had been brought in, and lay stretched out on the floor. Other refugees were huddled around.

Gently the boys laid Roland down. Paul rolled up his

jacket to serve as a pillow and Carlo and Gaston spread theirs over him.

"I should get home," said Paul. "Mother is alone."

Carlo and Gaston were equally worried about their families, but all hesitated to leave Roland.

A woman came over to them. "The doctor and the nurse will be here soon. I'll do what I can for your friend until then."

"You are kind," Paul told her.

"You're crazy to leave here," someone called as they started to go. "You'll be killed sure."

Outside, the nightmare was still being enacted. How long did the bombs fall? Perhaps twenty minutes in all. It was a small raid in comparison with many others, not even worthy of a few lines in a city newspaper. For those who were part of it, such comparisons were meaningless. They saw only the fearful destruction from the skies, which they were powerless to prevent, to halt, or to combat.

Paul felt the earth trembling beneath his feet as he raced toward home. Brief scenes of horror flashed out of the smoke and clouds of dust. It was so unreal he could not even be afraid.

"Mama!" A curly-headed baby girl with tears running down her cheeks, clad only in a nightdress, was standing in front of a mound of bricks which had once been a house. People were rushing by as unheeding as if she were a dirty-faced rag doll.

"Mama!"

Instinctively Paul knelt down beside her. "What's the matter, my little one?"

"I want my Mama," she sobbed.

"Where is your Mama?"

"There!" The child pointed to the bricks.

"Come now, she couldn't be." Paul stroked the dark curls. "Perhaps she's gone to the store. We'll try to find her."

The little one shook her head violently. "I won't. I won't leave Mama."

Could there possibly be anyone still living in that debris? Paul started clearing away the bricks. The child was close at his side.

"Mama!" she called over and over. "We're coming to get you."

Paul began to work feverishly, tossing bricks to the right and left. A passerby stopped, watching him.

"You there!" called Paul. "Give me a hand."

"No time," muttered the man, rushing off.

Paul did not bother to ask for help again. At last he caught a glimpse of a woman's skirt.

"There's my mama!" cried the child happily.

Paul straightened up, wiping his forehead with his hand. "I'll tell you what, my little one. Why don't you go across the street and sit down."

"No!"

The bombs had stopped falling but Paul hardly noticed. Finally he had freed the woman from the debris. Her head had been protected but bricks had been pressing on her chest and blood was coming from her mouth. She was breathing feebly.

"Mama!" Her small daughter was rubbing up against her like a kitten.

The woman opened her eyes and smiled slightly. "Be a good girl, Josette," she whispered. Then her head fell back limply and there was nothing more Paul could do. The child began to wail.

"Come, Josette." Paul picked her up in his arms. "I'm

taking you with me." He carried her, still sobbing, until he reached home.

The front door was off its hinges. He stumbled as he stepped inside. With the flashlight that the Nazis had fortunately left him, he surveyed the damage. All the windowpanes were broken. The cupboard in which his mother kept her best china had toppled over and the scattered fragments littered the floor. There were great cracks in the walls and ceilings. He went on into the kitchen but it was empty.

Now it was his turn to call. "Mother!"

"Is that you, Paul? I'm in the cellar."

He opened the cellar door just as his mother came up the stairs with two women neighbors.

"You're safe, Paul." Her eyes and her voice betrayed her anxiety.

How much more she would have worried, he reflected grimly, had she guessed the fate from which the bombardment had saved him.

"Here's something for you to look after, Mother." He thrust Josette into her arms. "Her mother was crushed to death. Tomorrow we'll find out who she is."

"Oh, the poor little one!" She was caressing the child, as he knew she would.

"I'll be back later." He headed toward the door.

"You're not going out again?"

"I must. If I had reached Josette's mother a few minutes earlier her life might have been spared. There may be others like her—for whom tomorrow will be too late."

"Haven't you done enough, Paul? Can't someone else take over?"

"No, Mother." That was one lesson he had learned from his work as a Patriot. One has never done enough.

Outside it was now very dark, and quiet too, except for occasional bursts of sobbing as someone came upon a loved one for whom he had been searching. At the end of the Coron, Paul found a rescue crew already at work.

"May I help?" he asked.

"We need every hand we can get, Paul."

He recognized the speaker as Jean-Luc, the young leader of the Moyelle Patriots. Most of the others in the crew were also Resistants. Paul felt a surge of pride that those who were working actively for France's liberation were the first to offer help in this emergency. Unlike the stranger who had called "No time" to him when he was trying to free Josette's mother.

"This one is alive." Two of the rescue crew had brought out a wounded man.

"Take him to the schoolhouse," ordered Jean-Luc. "Paul, you come with us. There's the Benoit house. The parents, seven children, and two grandparents lived there. Some of them may still be saved."

So it went all through the remainder of the night. Dawn came to reveal a town of desolation and sorrow. Frequently the crew's efforts were in vain but every so often they found someone trapped in the rubble who might not have survived had they arrived a little later. That was their reward. A strange woman gave Paul some coffee which he drank automatically without even thanking her. He was unaware of his own fatigue. Images of bricks, torn walls, broken furniture, swam in his brain and he only knew that they must keep on.

So changed was Moyelle that dreary gray morning that Paul did not realize they had reached the Du Bois house, a hollow shell of bricks and gaping windows.

"Yes," one of their crew was saying to Jean-Luc, "it was

the husband in this household who lost an arm in the First World War, only to be killed in this one by a dynamite explosion. Then the oldest son died in a mining accident. Alas, it would seem true that misfortune lives with some families."

They worked silently as they brought out the victims— the brave mother, with the baby Raymonde still clutched in her arms . . . Mark . . . Maurice . . . Marcelline . . . the twins, Gilbert and Gilberte. The whole family had been trapped in the kitchen as the roof gave way over them. The men of the crew stood with bowed heads. At first it seemed that Death had gathered them all, but suddenly little Raymonde let out a wail. The mother had held the youngest cradled in her arms to protect her, saving the child's life.

Then ten-year-old Mark stirred slightly. One of the men leaned over him. "This one is breathing!"

"Lucette!" Paul cried out suddenly. "Lucette must still be inside!"

"Ah yes, Lucette, the oldest," said one of the crew. "It is impossible!"

"She might be in the cellar!" Paul headed into the ruins.

"Stop, Paul," commanded Jean-Luc. "You can't go in there. The floor is ready to collapse. You'll be risking your life!"

But Paul was already scrambling down through the cellar door. The cellar ceiling was partially caved in, and he had to crawl over broken planks and other debris. "Lucette!" he called. "Where are you, Lucette?"

"Come back here, Paul!" It was Jean-Luc's voice in the distance.

Paul continued his frantic search, bruising his hands as he plowed through bricks, not even noticing when he tore his clothes and cut his legs on the nails from the jagged planks. Then there was a crunching, cracking sound, and he felt himself pinioned down by slabs of plaster. There was no pain. He simply was not able to breathe, though his lungs strained to the bursting point.

When he came to, he was lying on a cot in a big room crowded with similar cots. A Sister was leaning over him.

"There now, don't try to move, my boy," she said gently.

"Where am I?" Paul demanded.

"In the hospital at Lens, my child. You must not talk."

Paul started to raise himself up but a sharp pain in his ribs stopped him. Then he saw that his leg, bandaged until it was twice normal size, was sticking up in the air, attached to a sort of pulley. It looked funny, as though it did not belong to him at all. Uncontrollably, he began to giggle.

"Quiet, child." The Sister put her hand to his forehead.

"What's the matter with me, Sister? How badly am I hurt?" It seemed to him vitally important he should know the extent of his injuries.

"Nothing serious."

"Please tell me the truth, Sister."

"Yes, my little one. You have a crushed rib and a concussion. Your leg was broken."

"Will I be able to walk?" Paul asked anxiously.

"Yes, though not today or tomorrow," she told him. "You are fortunate. It looked very bad when they brought you here. One doctor was certain that the only way to save your life was to amputate your leg. But the second doctor disagreed. He said, 'This boy will need both his legs and I am going to see that he has them.' He spent nearly four hours on the operation. You will be all right now, as good as ever."

"That doctor . . . what is his name?" asked Paul. But he lapsed into unconsciousness before hearing the Sister's answer.

When he came to a second time, the doctor was beside him, the one with the rimless glasses and the hesitant manner whom he had known as Dr. Pinot, the same who had come again and again to the Chamber of the Underground to care for their wounded.

"How are you feeling, Paul?"

"All right, I guess."

"Sister, bring him some soup. I think he'll be able to take it."

"How long have I been here, Doctor?" Paul asked.

"About three weeks."

"And my mother?"

"She has been to see you. She will come again today."

There were so many other questions to which he needed the answers.

"Roland?"

"He was here for a day and then we released him. He was only stunned."

"Carlo and Gaston?"

"They are fine. They were doing rescue work in the Cité des Cheminots, as you were in the Corons, but they were not so rash as you. All three of your friends are in the country now. We felt it would be better for their health to get them out of town for a spell."

Then the Nazis had not picked them up again. He breathed with relief. He felt tired, fearfully tired, but there was one more thing he had to know.

"And Lucette . . . Lucette Du Bois?"

"She was away the night of the bombardment. I am told she was visiting a sick friend."

He knew what the doctor meant. Lucette had been on a mission. And that mission had saved her. Just as the bombardment had saved him and his friends from the Kommandant. How strange life was!

"Thank you, Doctor." His eyes closed.

"He's sleeping now," he heard the doctor say to the Sister as she returned with the soup. "But see that he takes it later. He is going to need plenty of nourishment."

He was not sleeping yet, just resting and thinking. He had all the time in the world for sleep now, as much as he wished. There would be no more nightly missions for him. The matter had been taken out of his hands.

CHAPTER *12*

ON THE FARM

"So, Paul, you've been eating my food for six weeks. Time you earned your keep. You can start by peeling potatoes for your aunt."

"Yes, Uncle. With pleasure." Paul smiled up at his Uncle Georges from the wheelchair by the window of the whitewashed country kitchen. "You've been good to me. I shan't forget it."

"Nonsense," snapped his uncle. He had just come in from the fields and was dressed in the patched denim trousers and faded blue shirt which had seen a dozen summers and hundreds of washings. "I did what I had to do. Get him the potatoes and a paring knife, Marie."

"Yes, monsieur," his wife said timidly. She was a tiny woman with a kindly wrinkled face, who always wore a black ankle-length dress and black cotton stockings. After forty-five years of married life, Paul's great-aunt still called her husband "monsieur," as though he were a stranger. Obediently, she fetched a large kettle of potatoes from the low cupboard where they were stored, though she neglected to bring the paring knife, an oversight which her husband failed to observe.

Paul was no longer afraid of him. Not after the way he had come storming into the hospital, demanding that the authorities release Paul in his care. He had just learned from Madame La Coque that the hospital had nothing but split-pea soup to feed their many patients. No nephew of his, he had proclaimed noisily and repeatedly, was going to be nourished on that ill-smelling stuff. Raging, he had gone through all the hospital formalities until he got what he wanted. Whereupon he had bundled Paul into the back of his wagon and left, stopping only to pick up Madame La Coque and the baby, Josette. They had all been at the farm ever since. The fare was plain but Uncle Georges actually seemed to enjoy making them eat.

Madame La Coque came in from the garden, carrying a basket of string beans she had plucked from the vines, and sat down by her son. In the few weeks they had been on the farm, her face had filled out and there was color in her cheeks. She was beginning to look young again.

"How beautiful it is out there," she said wistfully, "the sky so blue and the fields so green."

"You city folks," scoffed Uncle Georges. "You make a lot of money and spend it foolishly and in the end what do you have? Not even a piece of earth to call your own."

To Uncle Georges, Moyelle was a big city, like Lille or Paris, a place where "people spend all they earn for the clothes on their backs" and "have to borrow when the rent comes due." When old people have set notions like that, it is impossible to change their minds, and Madame La Coque, no more than Paul, did not try.

"You're right, Uncle," she agreed. "There's nothing like a farm of your own. I'd like to stay here the rest of my life."

"When your husband returns you'll sing another tune," Uncle Georges grumbled dourly. "You don't fool me."

"Look what we found, Mama!" Mitzi, closely followed by Josette, burst into the room, thrusting a bunch of wild flowers into her mother's lap. "Aren't they beautiful?"

"Hrumpf," snorted Uncle Georges. "They're only weeds."

"They are flowers," little Josette corrected him primly. Josette had turned out to be a pretty child, once she was washed and cleaned, with soft dark curls and big violet eyes. After the bombardment, they had learned that she was a Parisian. Her father had come from Paris to work in the mines as an alternative to going to Germany in a forced-labor battalion. But mining is a hard profession for one not brought up to it, and in his second winter he had succumbed to a severe attack of pleurisy. Josette's mother had stayed on in the company house until the bombardment. Madame La Coque had written to the Paris address which the mining company had given her, hoping to find some relatives, but so far there had been no answer. The tiny Parisian had become one of their family.

Aunt Marie picked up the half-wilted bouquet. "I'll put them in water so they will stay fresh." She filled a glass with water from the dipper and was arranging the flowers in it when Emile came romping in.

"The Germans are leaving," he announced. "Come take a look!"

"I've waited a long time for this," cried Paul. "Mother, would you wheel me outside?"

All of them, even Uncle Georges to whom wasted time was wasted money, went down to the gate to watch.

The Maquis had driven out the local German garrison a few nights before. These were the remnants, unshaven and gray, their uniforms shabby, their boots unpolished, making their exodus in lumbering wagons, high old-fashioned carts, whatever vehicles they had managed to confiscate in their haste to get away. Some were elderly, and some were boys hardly as old as Paul. A number wore rough and bloody bandages. All had a shamefaced beaten air, and they kept their eyes to the ground.

What had happened to Hitler's blond giants who had marched in so triumphantly? The best of them had been transferred to the Eastern Front, Paul had heard, where many had met their death. He watched in silence. It did not even seem worth while to jeer.

"There's work to be done," announced Uncle Georges, herding them back into the house.

The long-heralded Second Front, the invasion—on D-Day—of the Normandy Coast, had come while Paul was still in the hospital. Now Paris was a free city once again. Now it was only a question of time. . . .

"The Americans are coming!" A neighbor brought them that news later the same day. Uncle Georges, alerted by Emile, came up panting and stamping from the fields where he had been digging potatoes. Once again Madame La Coque wheeled Paul down to the gate. Mitzi and Josette pranced around in excitement. Aunt Marie, deserting her unwashed dinner dishes, rushed out, carrying the wild flowers which the children had picked earlier.

The distant sounds of motors grew louder and then they were there, the American troops in their trucks, big and strong, young and healthy-looking.

"*Vive l'Amérique!*" cried Madame La Coque. "*Vive les américains!*"

The others, even the two little girls, echoed her greeting, waving and shouting as the trucks went by. The Americans called back and some of them tossed down chocolate bars and cigarettes. Aunt Marie tossed her flowers up to them.

A tall young captain, standing on one of the trucks, caught the flowers and called, *"Merci beaucoup, madame."* As they passed, he shouted back, *"Moi, je suis français aussi —français-américain."* ("I, too, am French—French-American.")

Aunt Marie blushed as though she had made a conquest.

All too quickly the last of the trucks had gone by. While Josette and Mitzi were gathering up the chocolate and Uncle Georges was examining curiously the American cigarettes, Paul sat scowling in his wheelchair. He had imagined this meeting so often and so differently.

Why did the Americans have to see him in a wheelchair surrounded by women and children? He was a soldier, as they were. It was unfair. To his shame, on this day of their Liberation he found himself wanting to burst into tears.

"Mother, wheel me back to the kitchen," he said roughly.

That afternoon Emile went to town on an errand and came back ecstatic. Some of the Americans were bivouacked there, and they had let him wander all through their camp.

"You can't imagine what they were eating. Corned beef. Just like the cans we found in our courtyard."

"Poor boys," sighed Aunt Marie. "I wish I could have them here for dinner."

Paul felt worse than ever. Even his young brother had been allowed to make friends with the Americans.

"You're going to have a surprise, Paul," Emile said in a loud stage whisper.

"What?"

"I promised I wouldn't tell."

"Well, don't then." Paul turned away, ignoring the hurt look on Emile's face.

He did not have long to feel sorry for himself. About an hour later, Emile, suffocated with excitement, vanished out the door and started running down the road. In a few minutes he returned, escorting two khaki-clad figures. One of them was the same young captain who had caught the flowers thrown by Aunt Marie. The other, clad informally in fatigue trousers and a shirt open at the neck, was a tall gaunt man with familiar blue tattoo marks across his cheeks and forehead.

Paul's first thought was that this must be an American miner. Then with sudden recognition he cried out, "Felix!"

"*Bonjour*, Paul," said the miner, smiling at his astonishment. "Yes, it is I. Let me present my friend, Captain Ronald De Lisle from Maine, America, where people speak French too."

There were introductions all around. Aunt Marie kissed the captain on both cheeks, saying, "You are welcome here." The two little girls, petrified with admiration, stood motionless with their hands behind them. Emile pranced around with delight.

"Come in. Come in." Aunt Marie led the guests into the front parlor. "I will make you some coffee."

"Do you grind it in a coffee mill?" demanded the young captain.

"But of course. How else could one do it?"

"In America coffee comes in cans," the captain explained. "But my grandmother was French and always insisted that coffee had no taste or flavor unless it was ground by hand. Will you let me come out and watch you, madame?"

"If you wish, *Monsieur le Capitaine*." Aunt Marie was beside herself with embarrassment and pleasure.

While the captain was in the kitchen, Felix pulled up a chair beside Paul, to bring him up to date on recent happenings. Madame La Coque joined them. There was no need to keep secrets from her now.

Felix had been in Normandy on D-Day. In fact, his Resistance group had given assistance to the Allied invasion. That was when he had met Ronald De Lisle, the American captain. The week before, he had been in Moyelle, helping with the Liberation fighting there. After that was over, he had decided to take a vacation and come to see Paul. Quite by chance he had seen De Lisle in town and asked him to come along.

"I would have given anything to be in Moyelle and fight in the Liberation." Paul spoke enviously.

"You helped when the need was greatest, Paul," said Felix. "There were plenty of Liberation fighters. One of them—this will surprise you—was Monsieur Beaulieu."

"The Engineer?" Paul repeated incredulously.

"Yes . . . and bravely too. He killed a slew of Nazis before he was shot, and he died a hero."

"How I misjudged him!" Paul was silent for a moment.

"Roland, Carlo and Gaston all did their share, too," continued Felix. "You will be happy to know that the Germans never did find the ammunition cache, though they did considerable digging after the Chamber was blown up. The boys took us to it through the secret entrance in the bombed-out cellar. They send you their greetings, as do Mademoiselle Ricard and Lucette. Doctor Pinot is coming to see you soon. He thinks he will have you walking before too long."

Paul sighed happily. "If only Father were back, everything would be perfect."

"I know." Felix looked grave. "You must be patient,

Paul. The Allies still have a long way to go before they can set free the prisoners in deportation."

"I could wait forever if I could be sure he was alive and well," Madame La Coque cried out. "Is there no way of finding out, Monsieur Felix?"

He shook his head. "Not yet, madame. I am sorry. All we can do is wait. Wait and hope."

Hope, Paul repeated to himself with an old pain. Oh, Father, you would be here tomorrow if our hopes were sufficient to bring you! But he resolved then and there he would not stop hoping, no matter how long he had to wait.

The American captain came in from the kitchen, carrying a tray with small cups of black coffee and a plate of cakes. Aunt Marie was scolding him as though she were his mother.

"In France, men do not work in the kitchen, my captain."

"In America," he told her teasingly, "the men put on aprons and wash the dishes every night. How would you like that?"

"Don't put ideas into her head, young man," said Uncle Georges.

"I've invited the captain to dinner tomorrow," announced Aunt Marie. "Monsieur Felix, too. We're going to have a real French dinner, like before the war."

"Hrumpf!" Uncle Georges, sitting in his rocker, took a puff of one of the American cigarettes. "I suppose I will have to bring out the bottle of old wine I've been keeping for a special occasion."

"Indeed you will, monsieur," his wife informed him. "Maybe more than one bottle."

"What have you done to her, young man?" Uncle Georges demanded accusingly. "Once she would not have dared speak to me like that." Surprisingly, his voice was mild, as if he actually enjoyed his wife's attitude of independence.

The captain came over and sat down with Paul and his mother and Felix. "So this is the young man I've heard so much about," he said.

Felix nodded. "This is the one. Paul discovered the now legendary Chamber of the Underground, and he was a charter member of the Club of Young Patriots, a group of boys who did Resistance work when there were only a handful of Resistants in all of France. Under Paul's leadership, these boys continued their activities without letup throughout the Occupation until the night Moyelle was bombarded, when he was arrested. The arrest cost the lives of about a dozen German soldiers, since Paul had the foresight to set off a charge of explosives within the tunnel entrance to the Chamber. He escaped—and was wounded while working to save the lives of the bombardment victims."

The captain had certainly heard all this before, but Madame La Coque had not. She listened in wonder. "My Paul did all that?"

"I did not do it alone, Mother." Paul squirmed uncomfortably in his wheelchair. "We all worked together."

"Felix is proud of all of you," the captain said, smiling. "Tell me now. What was it like in Moyelle during the Occupation?"

Oddly enough, Paul could not think of a thing to say. All that had happened to him in Moyelle the last four years suddenly seemed quite trivial and unimportant compared to the thrill of the departure of the Germans, the reunion with Felix, and meeting his first American.

The Occupation? "It was not gay," he said finally. "It

was sad . . . and rather dreary. But would you tell me, *Monsieur le Capitaine,* that place Maine, where you come from, do you have Indians there?"

While the captain launched into a description of his own vast homeland, Paul settled back contentedly. At last he was to hear a firsthand report on the wonderfully exciting life in America!

EPILOGUE

Though France, if not the rest of Europe, was finally free of the Nazi invaders, there were still bread lines. There were still food shortages. An economy bled of all its riches could not be built up overnight. The mines, rid of their German directors, were nationalized, placed under government control, but money was lacking to repair the damages of four years of neglect.

Even before Paul's leg was completely healed, he went back to work, not in the pit but in the yard, sorting the coal from the slate and rocks as it was brought from the mine. Most of the sorters were girls; Paul felt like a sissy, working with women and doing women's work. He missed the camaraderie of the pit, particularly his long and intimate talks with Felix, and yearned for the time when the doctor would give him permission to dig coal with the men.

Following his return to Moyelle, there was an item in the town paper about the former Chamber of the Underground and the ancient tunnel leading to the Town Hall. Paul and his friends were given credit for the discovery. Two archaeologists from Paris heard about it and came to

Moyelle to see the tunnel for themselves. In their opinion, it had been built in the ninth century at the time that Norsemen had occupied the nearby city of Arras. It was possible that the citizens of ancient Moyelle, fearing a siege, had constructed this escape route. All the Germans of the First World War had done was to make a few repairs caused by water damage.

Even though the tunnel did not date back to Roman times, as Paul had hoped, the archaeologists considered it "an historical find of great importance." There was some talk of putting up a monument where the Chamber of the Underground had once been and even of setting up a guided tour through the tunnel. The plan was abandoned, or at least postponed, like so many others, for lack of funds.

Beginning in 1945, the mining company started a special school for its *galibots* to help them make up for the education they had missed. Paul and Roland and others like them attended two days a week, paid in full for their time. Morning classes were devoted to mathematics, electricity, and mining techniques. In the afternoon, they could take courses in French literature, composition, and history. Gymnastics were taught by a Swedish director whose very modern methods were designed to train all the muscles of the body. For Paul, in whom he took a personal interest, he gave special exercises to bring back movement to his stiff leg.

Though he made many new acquaintances, Paul's closest friends were still Roland, Carlo, and Gaston. The four boys gravitated to each other in peace as they had in war, but something was missing from their lives with the departure of the Germans. They had to admit it.

"It is as I thought it would be," Carlo said one day. "We

are no longer gangsters. We are respectable citizens. It is less frightening but it is also less interesting."

It was true. Learning to obey laws after four years of breaking them did not come easy. Many evenings Paul wandered restlessly around the small kitchen, not knowing what to do with himself, nostalgic for the old days, for the flavor of danger and the companionship of their secret meetings.

One Sunday night, on his mother's urging, he dressed up in his best clothes and went to the *Bal,* the dance which now, as before the war, was held once a week for the young people of the town at the Café Maxim. Standing on the sidelines with Roland, Paul saw Lucette, in a new dress, floating by in the arms of Jean-Luc, the former leader of the Patriots. At the intermission Paul got up courage enough to ask her for the next dance.

She smiled at him kindly and, it seemed to him, patronizingly. "Oh, I'm so sorry, Paul. I have every dance taken."

Wrathfully, he strode back to Roland. "Now she thinks she's too good for us," he muttered.

"She's just going through a phase," Roland said. "All women go through phases. In this one, Lucette likes older men. After all she's suffered, you shouldn't begrudge her that. Why don't you dance with someone else? I'm going to. There's a young girl over there with a very pretty nose and nice hair . . ."

"Go ahead," Paul grumbled. "Enjoy yourself. I'm leaving. This sort of thing is a waste of time."

Every so often the International Red Cross in Paris announced over the radio the names of the men deported from France who had been brought home. Listening to this broadcast was a combination of ecstatic anticipation and agonizing disappointment. "Jules La Coque! Jules La

Coque!"—the name Paul wanted most to hear rang so loudly in his ears that time and time again he thought he heard it when he had not.

Carlo's father had long since been released from Doullens and Gaston's had come back from the south of France where he had been working in the Maquis. Some of the concentration camp prisoners had returned too, terribly emaciated, often with but a little time left to live, but grateful beyond belief to be once more in the bosom of their families.

On May 7, 1945, Moyelle celebrated Germany's unconditional surrender, signed in Berlin. There was no work that day for anyone. Until late at night young and old danced in the streets, while accordions were played in every café in town. Paul shared in the festivities and was temporarily caught up in the jubilation, but left early, feeling strangely depressed. He came home to find his mother weeping.

"It's all over, Mother," he comforted her.

"I know," she said, and tried to smile. "It's just that everyone is so happy. Everyone else."

The next day they had a visit from a woman member of the Town Council. A well-meaning soul, she had taken it on herself to help the less literate citizens fill out the endless papers they needed to collect war pensions, compensation for war injuries, property damage from bombs, and so forth.

"Madame La Coque, I've come to suggest that you declare your husband dead," she announced tactlessly. "Then you will be eligible for pensions both from the mines and from the government, since Resistance fighters have been given the same status as other soldiers. In addition, your children will be declared Pupils of the Nation. As such, their tuition will be free and you will receive a special allowance for each of them up to the age of sixteen. I have brought the papers for you to sign."

"I can't do that," Madame La Coque said.

"But why not?"

"I do not believe that my husband is dead. It would be wrong for me to pretend that he was."

"As you wish." The woman left in a huff. It was obvious to Paul, who was present, that she had not expected to find such high scruples in the wife of a simple miner.

"Paul, did I do right?" Madame La Coque asked him afterwards. She spoke with difficulty. The woman's bluntness had been a cruel ordeal for her. "The money would help. There's no denying that. Perhaps I'm selfish. I should be thinking of Mitzi and Emile and of you. Even my saying that Jules is dead would not make him so, if he were not."

"We don't need money that badly, Mother," Paul told her firmly.

Later that day, Hélène Michel, Roland's mother, came to see them. She too had had a visit from the woman of the Town Council, urging her to declare her husband dead.

"I did not do it," she confessed. "I could not. Not yet. There was something too unbearably brutal about it. But sooner or later, Annette, we must face facts. We must realize how slim the chances are that we ever see our husbands again."

"I suppose you are right, Hélène," Paul's mother said, her voice dull and empty.

Roland's mother was not the same pretty and frivolous woman she had been at the time of Monsieur Michel's arrest. In those first weeks she had done nothing but sit home and feel sorry for herself. Then suddenly she had gone out and got a job as a servant to one of the railroad officials, arranging her hours so she could be home to give Roland his dinner. She had also become quite public-spirited. From the town's more prosperous citizens, even including some black-market profiteers, she raised money for Moyelle's war orphans. On Christmas and Easter she organized parties for the children, where they received gifts of cakes and candy and toys and were served refreshments.

Now it was Madame Michel, previously so helpless, who, dry-eyed, was urging Paul's mother to "face facts" and admit their husbands might not return.

Paul admired her new independence, but he could not stand to listen to such talk. He walked over to the window and looked out. It was raining and the grayness of the sky seemed to match the grayness of his mood. He thought back to that bright sunny day on Uncle Georges' farm, when Felix had said to him, "All we can do is wait and hope. . . . You must be patient, Paul."

"We must not lose hope." He turned to the two women. "Whatever happens, we must not stop hoping."

They looked at him, startled by the intensity of his voice.

On the morning of August 6, they had two more visitors, an elderly couple who introduced themselves as the grandparents of Josette. The man, who had a black beard and a scholarly look, explained that he was a science professor at the College of France. When the Nazis had tried to conscript his services to work on an explosives project, he and his wife had fled to the Savoy, a beautiful mountainous region in southwest France. Only recently they had re-visited Paris and found Madame La Coque's letter telling of the death of Josette's mother, their daughter. They were returning to the Savoy to spend their old age. Josette would be brought up in the country, with good mountain air to breathe and plenty of milk, butter, eggs and fruit for her diet.

They left, refusing to stay longer than to accept a cup of coffee, taking their small and bewildered grandchild with them. All afternoon, Mitzi wept loudly and could not be consoled for the loss of her friend. The others too felt they had lost a member of their own family.

That evening, about suppertime, Paul was listening to an International Red Cross broadcast and becoming more and more gloomy. There were very few new names of returned prisoners by this time. Most of the program was devoted to queries from persons like themselves, seeking to find someone returned from deportation who could give them information about a missing husband or father.

Suddenly the program was cut off in the middle of a sentence. "We interrupt for a special announcement," a voice said. The announcement had to do with a bombing raid by the United States on a Japanese city called Hiroshima. Only one bomb had been dropped in this raid, the announcer continued, but it was the most powerful bomb the world had ever known. He called it an atom bomb. This seemed curious to Paul, who knew from his reading that atoms were most exceedingly small.

"Do turn that thing off," Paul's mother called from the stove where she was frying potatoes. There was a note of irritation in her voice. "I'm sick of hearing about bombs and bombings. Haven't we had enough? It's time for supper, Paul. Pull up the chairs, Emile."

Since Josette had come to live with them, she and Mitzi had sat next to each other at mealtimes. Tonight, realizing that there was no place set for her tiny friend, Mitzi burst into wild sobs again.

"Why did they have to take Josette away?"

"Come now, don't cry," her mother tried to soothe her. "You're a big girl, Mitzi. We all knew that Josette was just paying us a visit. Now she has gone home."

But her daughter continued to weep, and finally Madame La Coque told her to pull up a chair and sit next to her, just as she had done when she was small.

She had her arm around Mitzi and was talking to her comfortingly, when Paul heard footsteps. Someone had come around the house to the back into their courtyard. Who could it be at this hour? It must be a friend or neighbor, since strangers would go to the front door. Whoever it was did not knock. With widening eyes, Paul saw the kitchen door open, very slowly as though the person outside was purposely postponing the moment when he would face them.

Then a tall haggard man with iron-gray hair stood in the doorway.

"It is you, Father!" Paul cried out.

His mother rose shakily, clutching at the table edge. Gesturing toward the chair which Mitzi had deserted, she said in a voice filled with sublime happiness, "Sit down, Jules. Supper is ready. We were waiting for you."

There was a tumultuous reunion after that. There were tears and laughter and embraces. There were snatches of confidences, mostly incoherent, and broken off by memories of things they had shared together. There were many questions and few answers. There was no mention of the "special announcement" over the radio, nor did Paul or his mother think of it. Not even the falling of the world's first atom bomb, of which neither had realized the significance in any case, could compare with the wonder of a father's return to his family.

Only later, after Emile and Mitzi had been sent to bed,

did Jules La Coque tell Paul and his wife why it had taken him so long to get home.

He had been at Oranienburg, as Mademoiselle Ricard's "friend" had reported, but toward the last had been transferred to Buchenwald, one of the worst of the German concentration camps. He and André Michel. The Americans liberated the camp—the date was April 13, 1945, he learned later—but at the time he was in a coma.

Weeks later, at the hospital to which the Americans took him, he regained consciousness but that was all. He did not know who he was, where he lived, where he had been. His memory returned slowly and spasmodically, in brief unrelated flashes—the train ride to Belgium when he was a child; his wife serving him soup; Mitzi laughing up at him; the big orange eyes of the cat Baboule staring at him from the darkness of the mine gallery.

What a job it was to find out his identity from these fragmentary glimpses. Worse than a jigsaw puzzle. The American psychiatrist had helped him. Then when he really started to remember, he almost wished he could sink back into oblivion.

"There were some things . . ." His eyes filled with a burning anger. "André. I couldn't face it. Remember how he used to be? Remember how strong he was and how his shoulders shook when he laughed? To see him grow weaker day after day. To sit by his side and watch his life leave him. To be helpless, utterly helpless to do anything about it. . . ."

He wept.

Paul saw the stricken look on his mother's face and searched vainly for some way to ease his father's anguish.

Poor Ronald! Poor Madame Michel! It was a good thing that she had become an independent woman, that she had steeled herself to "face facts." She would need all her new courage now.

"I'm glad you're home, Father," he said finally. And then somehow the older man recovered his composure and they talked of other things.

There was time in the days that followed to get re-acquainted with him. There was time to tell him all the things that had happened in his absence. There was time, too, to confide to him the lost feeling that had beset him the last months, the feeling that he had lived his life and that there was nothing worth while for him to do.

"But there is plenty to do, Paul," his father told him.

"You mean I must dig a lot of coal to make France strong again?"

"Not only that, my boy. I had time to do some thinking in the hospital—that is, when I began to feel well enough to think. The war is over, but the real struggle is still ahead. It won't be as simple as killing with bullets and bombs. The poison that caused the war is our enemy now. So that it will never happen again—so that André Michel, Du Bois, the little Jeannot, and all the others will not have died in vain—we must fight against prejudice, injustice, ignorance. We must fight for a better understanding among men. It will be a long battle and likely it will not be won in our lifetime. But at least you and I, together, can make a start. Are you willing to try?"

"Yes, Father," Paul said.

That he was not quite sure of his father's meaning, that he had little idea what he was expected to do, did not still his exultation. At long last his father had called on him. This time no "vicissitudes of circumstances" would inter-fere. On this mission, whatever it was, they would work together, father and son.

The Author

ROBIN McKOWN was born in Denver. She attended the University of Colorado, Northwestern University, and the University of Illinois. While still attending college she sold her first one-act play to a literary magazine. After college she worked in public relations, and prepared scripts for radio. Her many books for young people include biographies of Benjamin Franklin, Thomas Paine, and Marie Curie, all published by Putnam.